AND THEN THERE WAS YOU

SUZY TURNER

And Then There Was You

by Suzy Turner

Copyright Suzy Turner 2014
Published by Chill Out Press

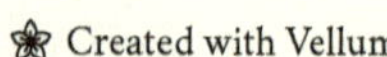 Created with Vellum

 # FREE DOWNLOAD 

Willow Tree Farm

Nestled among a thicket of weeping willows deep in the heart of Dartmoor, lies a house like no other. A house defying the laws of logic–and gravity for that matter. Some might even say it had a mind of its own. They wouldn't be wrong.

Affectionately known as Willow, this house has been an integral part of the Winterbourne family for over 400 years, and it is very, very protective of the Winterbournes, so woe betide anyone who dares to wrong this family of witches…

Compatible with all reading devices.

Exclusively available, and never before published.

Get your FREE COPY of Willow Tree Farm when you sign up to the author's VIP mailing list. **Get started here:**

www.suzyturner.com/free-book

PROLOGUE

It was so out of character for me. I'd never been unfaithful before, not to any of my childhood boyfriends and certainly not to my husband. But here I was, lying in a hotel bed with a complete stranger. My heart felt like it was being pulled apart – not because of the absolute guilt that filled me, but because of the strength of feeling I had for the beautiful man I'd just slept with.

The mutual attraction had been so raw and powerful. I was drawn to him instantly, as he was to me, it was easy to tell. The sex had been like nothing I'd ever experienced before, and I knew I'd probably never experience again. I was married. It was a mistake. I knew as I tiptoed out of his bed and out of his hotel room that I'd never forgive myself. I had slept with another man. It was unforgivable.

My husband was out of the country on one of his surfing weekends with his friends, and I was in London for a book signing. After the signing I'd resigned myself to an early night, but first, a light dinner in the hotel's cosy looking restaurant.

After my chicken salad I sat alone, gazing out of the window, enjoying the solitude with a glass of chilled white Chardonnay. I'd spotted him walk in. He sat down a few tables away and ordered a steak, medium rare, and a glass of white wine. Our eyes met, and I glanced away, blushing. The complete opposite to my tall, red-haired, well-built husband; he had dark hair, dark eyes and carried a little bit of excess weight, but was by no means fat. He was just a different build, more like a rugby player than a football player. He looked almost exotic somehow, yet he spoke with a clear English accent, perhaps with a slight west country twang?

I watched him whenever I could; I was so intrigued by him. I think he was doing the same to me. Whenever he looked up, I looked away, yet I could feel his gaze on me. My entire being tingled and eventually, I couldn't look away any longer. He smiled, making me want to melt into the chair. I finally smiled shyly back, and that's when he stood up and approached me.

'Hello.'

'Hi,' I replied, tucking my hair behind my ear.

'Would you mind if I joined you?'

I should have said yes, I should have made it clear I was taken. 'Not at all.'

He smiled again. It was incredible how the simple act of smiling could change a person's face. He was undeniably handsome. My body responded immediately, the warmth spreading lower and lower, working its way down my abdomen until... Well, until I blushed.

'I'm Adam.'

I couldn't help but chuckle. He tilted his head quizzically as he sat down across from me, I dropped my eyes before answering. 'Eve.'

Adam chuckled. 'Oh, I see.' He leaned forward, holding out his large hand; his long fingers reached towards me. I breathed in and held mine out in response. I knew what would happen because I'd felt the connection already. Electricity.

The second his skin touched mine a tingly feeling erupted from my fingertips, and we both gasped, pulling our hands away from each other abruptly.

Both of us blushed as the waiter approached.

'Would you like some more wine, sir? Madam?'

'That would be lovely, thank you.'

'Perhaps a bottle?' suggested Adam.

I smiled and nodded ever so slightly.

'Chardonnay?' asked the waiter.

'Yes that'll do fine, thank you.' I smiled.

'Are you here on business or pleasure?' Adam asked, once our glasses had been replenished.

'Business. And you?'

He nodded. 'Me too. What do you do?'

'I'm an author. I had a book signing not far from here.'

'That's very impressive,' he replied. 'What kind of books do you write? Romance? Horror?' He smiled.

'A little of this, a little of that,' I teased.

'A woman of many talents. I like that.'

I felt my cheeks darken. 'And you? What do you do?'

'Nothing nearly as exciting as writing books, I'm afraid.'

I raised my eyebrows and waited, taking a sip of wine.

'I'm into garden centres.'

'Oh?'

Adam nodded and grinned. 'I just sold one. I was here finalising all the paperwork with the vendor.'

'Well, congratulations on the sale, Adam,' I said, holding up my glass to his.

'Thank you. It's lovely to have someone so beautiful to celebrate with.'

I smiled, watching as his eyes caught sight of my wedding ring. His expression dropped a little.

'You have a family?' he asked.

'A husband, yes. No children, though. And you?' I looked down at his ring finger, which was devoid of any adornment.

'Two children – eighteen and twenty-one. Divorced about ten years ago.'

'Oh, I'm sorry.'

'Don't be. We're still friends, just weren't meant to be married, that's all. We've got two fantastic kids, though.'

'That's lovely. It's rare to hear of divorced couples who are still friends. Good for you. And your children? Boys?'

Adam's face lit up. 'The eldest is a boy and the youngest a girl. They're good kids. Both off studying at university. One's in Bournemouth, the other in Bristol.'

'That's lovely. I thought I detected a slight west country twang there.'

'Really? Most people can't hear it. I actually left when I was a youngster. I've lived all over the UK. I can't quite put my finger on your accent, though. Very, erm... British.' He chuckled, taking a swig of wine.

I laughed. 'Not many people can identify it. I was actually born in Yorkshire, but we moved abroad when I was a toddler. We did quite a bit of travelling around Europe, and my parents finally decided to stay in Portugal, but by that time I'd had enough and wanted to come back and make a proper home for myself. I was seventeen. That's when I met Matt, my husband,' I said, twirling my wedding ring around my finger.

'Ah yes, your husband,' Adam said quietly, circling his finger around the rim of his wine glass, making it hum. 'You've been together a long time then?'

I nodded. 'Twenty years.'

'That's nice.'

'Yes, I suppose it is.' I didn't know what else to say.

We both just sat there in silence, finishing the bottle, all the while, my heart fluttering in my chest. And the throbbing else-where only intensified. I knew I had to leave. I didn't want to, but I knew I had to force myself to leave this beautiful man behind.

'Well it's been a real pleasure talking to you, Adam,' I whispered as I slowly stood up. But the wine went straight to my head, and I stumbled ever so slightly.

He was up like a shot, steadying me. 'Are you okay?'

I couldn't answer him because his touch had rendered me speechless.

'Eve? Perhaps you should lie down. Let me help you to your room.'

Our eyes locked, and something unsaid passed between us and I slowly nodded.

CHAPTER 1

*S*lowly opening my eyes, I turned my head to see Matt snoring peacefully beside me. It was already half-past eight. I sat up, pushing the cat off the bed. She jumped straight back on and proceeded to walk all over my legs before she realised I was getting up and wouldn't be stroking her. Turning her attention to Matt, she stretched her limbs before pouncing on his chest.

'It wasn't me. I didn't do it,' Matt shouted, as his eyes fluttered open.

'Wasn't you? What didn't you do?' I asked, knowing full well he'd been dreaming.

'Huh?' he said, rubbing his eyes for a moment before stroking the cat for a few seconds. He then knocked her back onto the floor. She miaowed and stalked out of the bedroom in a mood.

'What were you dreaming about?' I asked.

'I wasn't dreaming.'

I raised an eyebrow. 'I think you were, you muttered something like, "I didn't do it. It wasn't me".'

'Really?' he asked. 'I don't remember. What time is it?'

'After eight-thirty.'

'What?' he jumped out of bed and scrambled about, trying to find something to wear.

'Relax. It's Saturday.'

'Already?'

Nodding as I put my yoga outfit on, I opened the curtains and peered outside. 'Looks like we're getting new neighbours.'

'Yes, I'd heard Linda had sold the place. It didn't take long. I wonder who the new owners are.'

'I can only see the movers at the moment, although maybe...'

Matt wandered over, smacking me on the bum as he leaned over me to get a good look. 'Maybe that woman there? She doesn't look like a mover,' he interrupted.

She was about my age – late thirties, with beautifully layered blonde hair almost down to her bottom – standing with one hand on her hip, wiping her forehead with the other. Every now and again, she'd say something to the gang of movers and laugh quite loudly. Her smile lit up her face. I don't know why, but I had the feeling that we were going to become friends.

'She looks nice,' I said, as I dropped the curtains. Matt held it open a little longer, watching everything that was going on in the street below. 'Cup of tea?' I asked.

'Mmmm, yes please, darling. I'm just going to hop in the shower. Don't suppose you want to hop in with me?'

'I'm going to do yoga first. Why don't you wait?'

'Can't, I'm afraid. I'm biking with Howard in half an hour.'

'Maybe this afternoon, then?' I asked as I walked past.

'Saturday afternoon nookie with my beautiful wife? It's a date.' He grinned, pretending to bump and grind. I shook my head and skipped down the stairs.

oOo

LYING on the bed wearing nothing but my favourite black lace thong and a black feather boa around my shoulders, I waited for Matt to walk into the bedroom. Remembering the music, I shimmied across the enormous four-poster bed and pressed play. The sounds of Madonna's Justify My Love filled the room. Just as I was shimmying back to the centre of the bed, Matt appeared with the biggest grin on his face.

'Wow,' he growled, throwing off his t-shirt and undoing the

buttons of his jeans before ripping off his socks, leaving nothing but the pink and red floral boxer shorts I'd bought him for Christmas.

'You can whip those off too, while you're at it,' I growled back.

Doing as he was told, he crawled over the bed and started kissing my neck before gently nipping at my ear. His hands roamed all over me, his mouth slowly moving lower and lower. My skin began to tingle, my body starting to throb precisely where I wanted it to, and I closed my eyes, remembering back to three years ago when I'd done something I shouldn't have. I'd tried to forget, but it was impossible. Every time Matt touched me, all I could think about was Adam. It had been just one night. One amazing night – the best sex I'd ever had. I tried to put it behind me, forget about it, but when Matt touched me, it was all I could think of. What I did was wrong, but at the time, it had felt so right.

A deep moan escaped my lips, and I grasped and pulled at the duvet with my fingers. But before I could come, he stopped and lifted his head, moving above me, toying with me before he thrust deep inside me. It took a minute until we were moving in harmony, the four-poster gently swaying against the wall when the sound of the doorbell rang.

'Shit,' Matt muttered.

'Just ignore it,' I said.

'No, it might be important.'

'More important than this?' I cried. 'Just leave it,' I urged, but he'd already climbed off and was throwing on his clothes.

'Babe, come back to bed. Whoever it is can wait.'

Matt turned and smiled. 'We can wait.' He winked before disappearing from the room.

I turned down the music and listened. When I heard the sounds of laughter, I threw on a pair of jeans and a vest and tiptoed to the top of the stairs. Leaning forward, I saw a mass of blonde hair disappear into the kitchen.

'... a glass of wine,' I heard Matt say.

'Ooh, yes, please. That sounds lovely, thanks.'

'Darling!' Matt yelled after a few seconds.

'Yeah?'

'Come and meet our new neighbours.'

'Shit,' I whispered. 'I'll be right down.'

Rushing back through our bedroom and into the en-suite, I looked at myself in the mirror. I was flushed, but it gave me a nice colour, I supposed, so I quickly applied a touch more mascara and eyeliner and ran the brush through my hair. I took a deep breath, smiled, and ran down the stairs.

We had quite a large kitchen diner, and when I walked in, there was nobody there. That's when I realised the back door was open. Matt must've been showing them around the rear garden. I poured myself a glass of wine and went to put the bottle back in the fridge, but when I turned back around, I bumped into someone.

'Oh shoot,' I whispered, narrowly missing throwing my wine all over him. I was so focussed on balancing my glass that I barely got a look at his face. But I knew. I knew before I saw him. I felt it, that connection.

I knew the man standing in my kitchen was Adam. Closing my eyes for a second, I took a slow, deep breath and lifted my face to his.

'Eve,' he whispered.

I shook my head. 'No,' I whispered, the air completely knocked out of me.

'Ah, I see you've met Adam,' Matt's voice boomed from the garden.

I stepped forward. 'Yes, Adam. It's lovely to m-m-meet you.' I nodded, shaking his hand. The second we touched, shivers rippled down my spine.

'Hello darlin',' said the gorgeous blonde I'd watched unload all their belongings earlier that morning. Holding out her hand, she bounded towards me. 'I'm Charlie. We did have a giggle, just now, when your Matt told us your name is Eve, considering my husband is Adam.' She laughed. 'Are you alright, my love? You look like you've seen a ghost.'

I shook my head and then nodded. 'No, no, I'm fine. Just feeling a little faint, that's all. I think I must've stood up too fast or something.'

'You sure? You look quite pale, darlin',' she said in a strong East London accent.

'No, honestly. I'm fine. Nothing that a glass of wine won't help,' I said, turning my attention to the wine in my hand. I took a sip, then a glug. Oh, what the hell; I downed the lot.

'Babe?' Matt asked, walking towards me. 'Sure you're alright?'

I smiled the biggest smile I could muster. 'Absolutely. Perfectly. Utterly fine. Don't worry. Fine, fine. I'm really, rather quite… fine.'

He looked at me as if I were off my trolley and nodded before he turned his full attention back to Charlie. 'You mentioned bikes, Charlie. Are you a biker?'

Charlie grinned. 'Ooh yes, I love bikes. But do you mean bicycles or ones with engines? Because I do love them both.' She giggled.

'Funny you should mention that,' I answered, 'because Matt loves them both, too. He's got a few.'

'Would you like to see them?' he asked, always eager to show off his two-wheeled specimens to anyone who showed him the least bit of interest.

'I'd love to,' she squealed.

'Follow me,' Matt said, with a huge grin.

I sighed as they exited the kitchen and headed towards the garage, thinking I was alone. Which I was, all for five seconds, before Adam walked back in and sat down beside me. 'Eve? Are you okay?'

I shook my head and poured myself another glass of wine. 'This was never meant to happen. I was never meant to see you again. And now we're neighbours, Adam. Neighbours. How did this happen?' I avoided his gaze for as long as possible, but I couldn't hold it for any longer, and I tipped my head towards him. My body wobbled; I mean, visibly wobbled. And he noticed.

He smiled and nodded. 'I feel the same as you, Eve. Really I do.'

'Really, Adam? But you weren't married,' I said, through clenched teeth.

'I was very nearly married.'

'Oh,' was all I could say.

'It was very irresponsible what we did, but we couldn't help it.

We had such a deep, intense connection. You can't control feelings like that.'

'And now?' I looked down.

'You're feeling it too, aren't you?'

'Of course I am. How can I not?' I looked up into those dark eyes and saw me in them. It wasn't just me that felt this way. He felt it too. I could see it.

'We can't see each other. We have to stop this before...' I whispered.

'I know. But we're neighbours. And how would we explain that to our partners? I presume you didn't tell...'

'Of course I didn't. As far as Matt's concerned, I've always been a faithful wife. It would kill him to find out that I haven't been. That I slipped up, just once.'

'Slipped up? Is that what it was?' Hurt filled his face.

'No, Adam.' I moved the wine out of the way on the table and, before I could think about what I was doing, my hand reached for his. The shock was instant, and my heart felt like it had been hit by lightning. 'Oh God, I can't believe this is happening.'

'I know, Eve. I know.' He slowly leaned forward and brushed his fingers down my cheek. 'We'll work it out.'

His touch was like shockwaves running through my body, and I jumped up out of my chair, stepping away from him. 'Please don't touch me, Adam. It's not a good idea.'

'I...I'm sorry. I couldn't help myself. But I won't, I won't. Not again. I promise.'

'Promise? Promise what?' asked Matt, as he and Charlie wandered back into the kitchen, both grinning like Cheshire cats.

'You should see his bikes, Adam. He's got one motorbike, two road bicycles, and a mountain bike.'

'Oh, really? That's quite impressive. I'm not much of a biker myself,' Adam said, turning his attention to our spouses.

'Well, we'll have to change that. Now that you're living next door, we'll have to go out together. Oh, and speaking of going out, Charlie and I were talking about going out for curry tomorrow night. Are you up for that?'

'*D*on't you think it's a bit soon to be going out for dinner with them?' I asked, hoping he might reconsider.

'Huh? Don't be ridiculous, Eve. How do you expect to make friends with the neighbours if you don't want to go out for dinner with them?'

'It's not that I don't want to go out with them, it's just that... that...' I paused; I didn't know what to say.

'Eve, you're weird sometimes, you know that?' Matt replied as he stepped out of the shower and began rubbing himself down with a towel that was clearly too small for the job. I walked out and grabbed a fresh bath sheet from the airing cupboard and returned, handing it to him. 'Thanks. C'mon, you'd better get ready, or we'll be late.'

'I...I think I've got a headache coming on.'

Matt glared at me. 'No, you don't. Don't you like them or something?'

'No. I mean yes, of course. Charlie is fun. Don't really know much about Adam, though.'

'He seems like a cool guy, now put some clothes on and do your hair.'

'What's wrong with my hair?' I asked, standing in front of the bathroom mirror, wiping it and looking at myself. My dark waves hung down past my shoulders.

'Nothing,' he answered. 'It's just nice when you do stuff to it, that's all.'

'Like what?' I rarely did anything with it.

He shrugged. 'I dunno. Something.'

'Don't you like it like this?'

'Sure... for every day. But for going out? I like you to make an effort.'

'An effort? I always make an effort.'

He raised his eyebrows and walked out of the bathroom.

'Whatever,' I whispered, as I forced myself to follow him, flopping onto the bed.

'Eve, for God's sake. Pull yourself together and get dressed. Have you seen my blue shirt?'

'Which one?'

'My favourite.'

'What? The midnight blue one? You're going to wear that tonight?'

'Why not?'

'It's just a curry at the local restaurant with our neighbours.'

'Yeah, and? What's wrong with wearing my favourite shirt? Just forget it. Have you seen it?'

'It's in the ironing. I'll go and press it for you.'

'Look, I'll do it myself. You go and get ready. We're leaving in twenty minutes,' he huffed, giving me one of his stares.

Holding up my hands in defeat, I stood up. 'Okay, okay.'

'Finally,' he muttered as he pulled the bedroom door closed behind him.

Standing in front of the full-length mirror, I dropped the towel to the floor and looked at my naked self.

Why the hell was this happening? Of all the streets in all of England, why did he choose this one? Just thinking about him made my body tingle. I put my hand to my chest and sighed. The hairs on the back of my neck were standing on end. Why had I done it? Why had I slept with him three years ago?

Because you couldn't resist him, replied the devil on my shoulder.

Yeah, but you're married, said the angel on the other side.

And you're still drawn to him, whispered the devil, and you want to make love to him, over and over and over.

Butterflies in my stomach fluttered as I turned away, trying so hard to remove that thought from my head. You're married, Eve. You're bloody married. Happily married, I might add.

Yes, repeated the devil, but Matt doesn't make you feel like Adam did. You think of Adam every single day. And why is that?

I growled at myself and shook my head. 'Stop it!' I practically yelled at myself.

'What's that?' shouted Matt from the next bedroom.

I felt my face turn pink. 'N-nothing.'

'Fifteen minutes, okay?'

'Yeah, I'll be ready soon.'

oOo

THE MOMENT I stepped through the door, I felt his eyes on me. Trying to avoid his gaze, I focussed my attention on Charlie.

'Hey darlin',' she smiled, approaching with her arms out in front of her before she kissed both my cheeks. 'You look smokin' hot.' She winked. Her tight skinny jeans emphasized her impressive curves, while my boyfriend jeans and white shirt did little but hide my own body. Matt hadn't been particularly impressed with my choice of outfits, so I'd put on a chunky necklace and a pair of heels to make him happier.

'Thank you. You look amazing, those jeans look incredible on you,' I replied, as she grinned and moved across to Matt. I couldn't help but notice his eyes settle on her bum when she turned to climb into the car. I rolled my eyes as Adam shook hands with Matt.

'Eve, you look lovely,' he said. I smiled and air-kissed his cheeks. We didn't even touch, and I could still feel my breathing quicken with every heartbeat.

'Thanks. Erm, you too.'

Matt had already climbed into the front seat and was talking animatedly with Charlie as Adam held the door open for me.

Feeling his gaze bore into me, I finally looked up at him and melted. Just looking into his eyes took me back to that night in the hotel. It felt like it was yesterday.

'I'm sorry about all this,' he mouthed.

I grimaced and smiled at the same time but said nothing. I just sat down beside his wife and put on a brave face. I looked from her to Matt and back again. If only they knew the truth. That her husband had fucked me every which way possible.

And it was bloody fantastic, said the devil on my shoulder.

I gulped and turned to look out the window, watching as the street lights suddenly turned on, like Adam had turned me on...and was still turning me on to this day.

'Are you okay, babe?' asked Charlie as she patted me on the hand. 'You look like you've seen another ghost or something.'

I shook my head. 'No, no. I'm fine.'

'You sure?' she asked.

I nodded. 'Yes, I was thinking about the book I'm writing, that's all.'

'Oooh yes, Matt told me you write books for a living. I'd clean forgotten you were an author. Anything juicy?' She laughed.

'No, not really. Not at the moment.'

'Tell them what you're working on,' Matt said, turning to look at me. He seemed to be desperately trying to include me in the conversation.

I smiled at him. 'Just a book for kids, at the moment. Nothing you'd be interested in, I'm sure.'

'Nonsense,' said Adam, from the driver's seat. 'We'd love to know what it is that you write. What kinds of things get you excited, I mean in the literary sense.' I could almost hear him curse himself under his breath.

But before I could say anything else, Matt had already changed the subject. Yeah, he really wanted to include me in the conversation, didn't he? I hated it when he did that. Adam looked at me, apologetically through the rearview mirror as we pulled up outside the Indian restaurant.

Matt climbed out first and opened the door for Charlie, who was sitting behind him.

'Thanks, darlin'.' She smiled.

Adam clumsily opened my door, and I rushed out, avoiding his stare and his touch. 'Thanks,' I muttered, as I quickly walked to Matt and let him put his arm lazily across my shoulder.

'It's a good job we booked,' Matt said as he dropped his arm and opened the door for us all. 'It's packed.'

Led to the only table left next to the window, we all sat down, Charlie talking animatedly about something I hadn't entirely caught.

'...don't you remember, Eve?' Matt asked.

'Huh?'

He glared at me. 'Charlie was just talking about their last holiday, to Las Vegas.'

'Oh, really?' I replied, looking towards her.

'I was telling them about our trip,' he said.

'Yes, yes, of course. We went in, what was it? Last January?'

'January?' Adam interrupted. 'That's when we were there.'

'Oh what a coincidence,' Matt smiled. 'Where did you stay?'

'The Bellagio.'

'No way, that's where we stayed.'

'Oh my God,' Charlie squealed. 'We were there together. That's just too weird. Did you like it?'

I nodded. 'Loved it. It was amazing.'

'I agree.' Adam smiled. 'It's one of those places that you have to visit at least once in your life.'

Matt laughed. 'Eve is always saying that.'

I reddened.

'Did you go to the canyon?' Charlie asked.

'Yes, but we got lost on the way there. The bloody GPS took us about two hours in the wrong direction.' Matt laughed, taking a swig of lager before continuing. 'And when we eventually got there, we were ripped off.'

'Really?' Charlie asked, leaning forward on her elbows.

'Yes, we had to get a coach, and then...'

I zoned out. I'd been there with him and had heard the story a million times before. I sat back and took a long sip of white wine.

'So what did you love the most about Vegas?' Adam asked

quietly, leaving our spouses to chat animatedly about our trips to the canyon.

I shrugged and smiled. 'Everything. The fact that each hotel is like a mini-city, the shows, the buzz in every casino, the food, the general atmosphere, the craziness of it all.'

'There must be one thing above all else that you remember,' he encouraged.

Smiling, I rested my arm on the table and put my chin on my hand. 'Hmm...' I sighed as thought. 'The Bellagio fountains were pretty incredible.'

He nodded. 'Amazing, weren't they?'

I nodded. 'Did you have a cocktail in the Bellagio bar?'

'Yes! They were wonderful,' he said.

'It wasn't just the drink though, but the ambience there with the guy playing the piano. It was very memorable.' I blushed, thinking about something else that had been far more memorable.

As if reading my mind, Adam choked on his lager.

'You alright, honey?' Charlie asked, temporarily halting her conversation with Matt.

Adam nodded. 'Fine, I should swallow the drink and not inhale it.' He grinned.

Charlie smiled and returned her attention to my husband.

'So where else have you been on holiday?' I asked.

'We went to New York,' Charlie answered. 'Oh my God, now that was amazing. What a city,' she breathed into her drink.

'Yes, it is,' I said.

'You've been?' asked Adam.

'We were there... a year before Vegas, I think.'

'Really?' Charlie asked.

We both nodded.

'What month?' Adam asked, curiously.

'When was it, darling?' Matt asked me.

'Late December.'

'No way,' Charlie whispered.

'What?' Matt asked.

'We were in New York then, too.'

'Really? Now that is a coincidence. I prefer beach holidays

myself, though.' Matt smiled, finishing his lager and asking the waiter for another. 'Anyone else for a refill?'

Adam nodded. 'Yes, please.'

'That'll be two pints of lager, please.'

'So where did you stay in New York?' asked Adam.

'A little place called erm… oh, what was it called, Eve?'

'The Hudson. Lovely place. I'd definitely go back.'

'The Hudson? The Hudson Hotel?' Charlie asked.

Matt nodded. 'You didn't stay there too, did you?'

Adam shook his head. 'No, but we were only round the corner from it.'

'Wow, it's certainly a small world, isn't it?' Charlie asked.

I glanced sideways at Adam and couldn't resist a smile. A small world? She had no idea.

CHAPTER 3

*A*dam and Charlie had been living next door for only a month and, other than the night we'd gone out for dinner, I'd managed to avoid him. Luckily, whenever Charlie had invited us out, we had been engaged elsewhere.

But I wasn't able to avoid them forever, and their house warming party was looming.

Sitting in my little office in the spare bedroom, I was supposed to be writing, but my thoughts were otherwise engaged. I could hear Matt whistling as he opened the front door. 'I'm home,' he yelled at the foot of the stairs.

'I'm working. I'll be down soon.'

'Okay, I'm going to mess around in the garage for a bit.'

'Knock yourself out,' I muttered. Some dutiful wife I was. I didn't even go and say hello properly. Not a kiss, nothing. Mind you, it's not like he was offering it to me either, was he? What was happening to us?

You're growing apart, said the devil on my shoulder.

But you can fix it, replied the angel.

How? A sudden picture appeared in my head, and I smiled. That would be nice. A bit of afternoon sex was always good for the soul. Grinning, I closed my laptop and headed for our bedroom. Opening my wardrobe, I rifled around until the box came into view. Taking off the top, I pulled out a couple of possible outfits. I wasn't in the mood for leather or PVC, so I settled on my favourite little lace number. It was actually a dress but was far too transparent and super short to be worn anywhere other than the bedroom. I grinned and closed the wardrobe door, undressing as fast as I could.

With the dress and stockings on, my hair up and lashings of black mascara, eyeliner and deep red lipstick, I smiled at my wicked self in the mirror. Grinning, I grabbed my little black satin dressing gown and threw it on before I skipped down the stairs. Taking a deep breath, I opened the door to the garage and seductively draped myself in the doorway, letting the gown fall open.

Unfortunately, Matt wasn't alone.

'Erm... babe?' he said, horrified, as I looked around and noticed Charlie straddling his motorbike.

'Oh,' I shrieked and pulled the gown tight around my body, as Adam came into view from behind the car. 'Oh shit,' I said, my face turning the deepest possible shade of red.

'Charlie and Adam just popped over to make sure we were going to the party tonight, seeing as you forgot to confirm,' Matt said, totally embarrassed.

He was embarrassed? Jesus.

'Oh, erm. Sorry. Yes, of course we'll be there,' I muttered. 'Must go and erm... turn the oven on.'

'What?' Matt said, through clenched teeth.

Grimacing, I quickly turned around and shut the garage door behind me.

Holy shit.

As I ran up the stairs, I heard the door open and close behind me.

'What the hell are you doing?' Matt said at the bottom of the stairs.

'I, erm, I... thought you might like to... Oh, it doesn't matter, anyway.'

'Babe, you can't just open the door to the garage dressed like that. Jesus. Talk about embarrassing. The whole neighbourhood will be talking about it.'

'Who gives a shit about the whole fucking neighbourhood?

What about me? I was hoping to have sex with my husband, that's all. Is that so wrong? How was I supposed to know they were in there with you? You normally keep the main door closed, unless you're going out.'

There was a knock on the garage door, and it was opened gingerly. Charlie popped her head around. 'Hello?' she said, looking around. When she spotted us on the stairs, she smiled. 'Please don't be embarrassed, darlin'. We're going to go. We figured you'd want to be alone for a while.' She winked.

'Oh no, there's no need to go,' Matt said, walking back down the stairs.

What the fuck?

'Really?' I muttered under my breath and turned around awkwardly, tripping clumsily on the top step before disappearing into the bedroom.

I heard them talking, and then the garage door closed behind them.

Well, screw you, Matt.

I threw myself on the bed and looked at the ceiling. I'd just revealed myself, in all my sexual regalia, to Charlie and Adam. Adam. Oh God. I turned on to my stomach and thought about the look on his face when I saw him standing there.

It wasn't embarrassment. He wasn't mortified. He was turned on. It was written all over his face. Oh God.

I bounced off the bed and walked over to the window. Adam was slowly walking back to his house alone. He turned to look at our place, and his gaze slowly turned upwards. I watched as he looked from window to window until his eyes eventually locked with mine. I wanted to turn away, but I couldn't. We just stood and stared at each other until I managed to tear myself away. I pulled the curtain closed and caught sight of myself in the mirror. Horny, God did that man make me feel horny. I couldn't help myself. My fingers tenderly brushed against my body as I imagined him rushing into the room, like some kind of knight in shining armour, and having his wicked way with me right there on the floor.

The idea caused shockwaves to reel through my entire being, and I barely had to touch myself before I came, sobbing quietly.

oOo

I PURPOSEFULLY PUT the quiche in the oven late; I didn't want to be early to the party. I wanted everyone else to get there first, so I could quietly walk in and blend in with the crowd.

Sitting beside the oven reading a book, I barely looked up when Matt walked in whistling. 'Oh, how long is that going to take?'

I looked up and noticed he was wearing a shirt I hadn't seen before. 'About half an hour.'

'But we'll be late.'

I shrugged, and he scowled at me.

'I haven't seen that shirt before.'

'It's new. I bought it today.'

'Oh, haven't you got enough shirts already?'

'I saw it in the shop window and liked it. Is that alright with you?' he asked sarcastically.

'Of course, it is. You buy whatever you want. You always have, anyway.'

'What's that supposed to mean?'

'Oh nothing,' I muttered and returned my attention to the book, which I wasn't really into. I was too busy thinking of other things. Of other people. Person.

When had we become this horrible bickering couple?

I sighed and put the book down. 'I'm sorry, darling. Look, why don't you go over to the party. I'll be over as soon as the quiche is ready,' I said, standing and pulling him towards me.

He put his hands on my shoulders and looked down at me. 'You sure?'

'Absolutely.'

'Okay. Shall I take the bottle of wine?'

I nodded. 'The shirt looks good, by the way.'

He smiled. 'You don't look so bad yourself.'

And with that, he was gone. A couple of years ago, he wouldn't have dreamed of going to the party without me. When had things changed? Was it since Adam?

Deep down, I knew things hadn't been right between us for some time. It must have been before Adam; otherwise, I would never have done what I did, would I? What we did, I corrected myself. It was Adam too.

Sighing, I looked at the quiche in the oven. Another twenty minutes or so. Standing up, I opened the fridge and pulled out the open bottle of wine. Taking a glass from the cupboard, I poured myself a large one and took a long gulp. As it slid down my throat, I could feel my muscles relax. I'd been tense since they'd moved in next door. I needed a massage; that would help. But first, I'd finish the wine and go and show my face at the party.

A knock at the back door made me jump, and I spilt a little wine on the floor, but I ignored it to go and see who it was.

Standing there, looking smoking hot, was Adam.

I swallowed, took another big swig of the wine like some kind of crazy housewife with an alcohol problem, and opened the door.

'What are you doing here?' I asked abruptly. 'Sorry, I'm just a bit tense...'

'Don't worry, Eve. I know exactly how you feel.'

'Really? Jesus... I'm so sorry. I don't know what's come over me, lately.'

'I do, I know exactly what it is.' He smiled apologetically. 'I am entirely to blame.' He looked down, and I stepped backwards.

'Come in. I'm just waiting for the quiche to bake. Would you like some wine? Or a lager?'

'Sure, a glass of wine would be great. Charlie sent me over to make sure you were okay.'

'She did?'

He nodded. 'She was worried you wouldn't come because you were... erm...'

'Embarrassed, mortified, horrified at being seen in my sexiest outfit?' I asked blushing.

'Well, yes, not that you have anything to be embarrassed about. I've seen you in less.'

'Adam,' I choked. 'Please don't mention that.'

'I...I'm sorry. I'm trying not to think about it, but it's proving somewhat difficult, especially after earlier.'

I wished I could stop blushing. I turned to look at the quiche instead.

'Are you happy, Eve?' he asked out of the blue.

I turned to face him. 'What do you mean? Of course, I'm h-happy,' I stuttered. 'Are you?'

He nodded and then shook his head.

'No, Adam. Please don't answer that. And please don't ask me that, either.'

He nodded just as the oven timer went off.

'Well, it looks like it's ready,' I said, picking up a tea towel as Adam went to pick it up.

'Let me,' he said, as our hands clashed, and before I knew what was happening, we were in each other's arms, kissing passionately. I felt like I was going to explode, feeling his tongue exploring my mouth like that as if he'd never been there before.

I got swept away in the moment, but after another minute, I managed to pull away.

'Eve, I'm so...so sorry. I hadn't planned to do that. I couldn't help it. Something tugs at me every time I'm near you. Damn it.'

I fell backwards and leaned on the countertop, breathing heavily. 'I...I...know. I feel the same, but we're married, Adam. We can't do this. Think of Charlie and Matt.'

'Don't you think I haven't thought of them? But Eve, you don't understand, I've thought of you every day since we first met. I haven't been able to get you out of my head.'

I raised my eyebrows. 'But you still got married?'

He took a deep breath and leaned beside me, handing me my wine and taking a large gulp of his own before he added, 'It was a month before the wedding, Eve.'

'What was?'

'Me and you.'

'Oh,' I said, looking at my feet.

'I couldn't break it off because of a one night stand. I thought I'd eventually forget you and I'd be able to be happily married to Charlie...'

'Aren't you? Happily married, I mean?'

He shrugged. 'I guess so. I mean, no. How can I be happily

married when all I can think of is you?'

'Some people can feel that way about more than one person, you know.'

He nodded sadly.

'If only things had been different, eh?' I said as I finished off my wine and turned back to the oven to remove the now slightly over-done quiche.

'I know. If you hadn't been married... If we'd both been single... Who knows.'

'But we are, Adam. We're both married, and we can't forget that now. That kiss just now. That can't happen again.'

'I know, Eve. I know,' he said sadly, as he placed his empty glass in the sink and walked over to the door. 'You ready?'

I nodded. 'Not really, but I guess I'll have to be. Oh, just a minute. Need to feed the cat,' I said, as I noticed her run indoors when he opened the door.

I put down some biscuits for her and picked up the quiche, sighing heavily. If only we could stay here and forget about the rest of the world, I thought, but I didn't say it out loud. Something told me, though, that he was thinking the exact same thing.

oOo

WE CREPT in through their back door, so nobody made a fuss about me as I placed the quiche on the dining table. Adam poured me another glass of wine, which I accepted gratefully with a long sad look before he disappeared to continue with his hosting duties.

I wandered into the beautiful living room, where a large crowd were busy chatting, and some were dancing discreetly to the jazz music blaring from the iPod dock in the corner by the huge TV.

I made small talk with some of our other neighbours before wandering out into the garden, where strings of fairy lights hung from various trees. I smiled. I loved fairy lights. In fact, I'd wanted to put some in our own garden, but Matt hadn't been keen. He had a habit of talking me out of doing little decorative things like that, which was probably why our house was so sparsely decorated.

Shivering as a soft breeze blew through the garden, I turned to see Charlie, looking stunning in a sequinned mini dress, walking down the stairs. She really was beautiful, especially when she was made up like that with her sixties-style lined eyes and her hair in something of a bouffant style. Matt was walking behind her, and they were talking animatedly and laughing.

I must ask for a guided tour too, I thought. It was a beautiful house. Very different in style to ours, which was quite traditional; theirs was very contemporary, with large windows everywhere. As I watched them through the window, someone tapped me on the shoulder. 'Excuse me,' said a middle-aged lady wearing a long woolly cardigan.

Smiling, I turned to her. 'Hello?'

'Hello, dear. Are you Eve Brooke, by any chance?'

'That's me.'

'Oh, how wonderful. I had heard you lived in the neighbour-hood but wasn't sure where. My daughter is a fan of yours. She's read all your books on her Kindle.'

'Oh, really? That's lovely,' I said, genuinely surprised. I'd never been recognised before, except at the few book signings I'd done, of course. 'I hope that means she's enjoyed them?'

'Are you kidding? She's always talking about them. She's a big fan. She even did a talk about them at school. Apparently, she got you lots of new fans.'

'Really? Wow, I'm really, very flattered. I must meet her and thank her in person.'

The woman grinned. 'She'd be absolutely delighted, I'm sure. I'm Gail, by the way. Gail Green. I can't wait to tell Emily.'

'I'm afraid I don't have business cards with me at the moment; otherwise, I'd give you one so you, or she, can call me. But I live next door, at number eighteen. You're welcome to drop by any time.'

'Thank you, dear. That's very kind. I'll tell her as soon as I get home. No doubt she'll still be up! Anyway, it's a little chilly out here. I'm going to head back in. Maybe see you later.'

I nodded as Gail disappeared indoors with a grin on her face.

'Accosted by the fans?' asked a voice from further down the garden.

'What are you doing down there?' I asked as Adam appeared out of the darkness.

'Just having some time out from the party. Are you having a good time?'

'Yes, I am, actually.'

'You sound surprised.'

I chuckled. 'I wasn't expecting to, to be honest.'

'I know what you mean.'

'I noticed Charlie gave Matt a tour of the house. I'd like to see it too if that's alright?'

'Of course.'

'Perhaps I should go and find her.'

Adam smiled. 'Yes, if you prefer.'

I rolled my eyes. 'I think it would be better that way.'

'What's that? What would be better?' asked a familiar voice from the large door that opened up from the living room.

'Hey, babe,' I said to Matt as he strolled towards us.

'I was just saying that I noticed Charlie gave you the grand tour earlier, and I'd like to see their place too.'

Matt nodded. 'Erm, yes. Adam, why don't you do the honours,' he suggested.

'Well, if you insist.'

'Are you coming?' I asked Matt, but he shook his head.

'Already seen it. I'm going to grab a lager. Enjoy.'

'Looks like we can't avoid it, then,' Adam whispered as he led me back indoors. The heat hit me, and I had to stop for a second to become accustomed to the temperature.

'Are you alright?' he asked me as he took hold of my elbow. 'You look like you might fall over.'

'No, I'm fine,' I said, gingerly extricating his hand from my arm and looking around shyly. 'Maybe this isn't such a good idea, Adam.'

'I'm sure we can resist each other's charms for ten minutes,' he whispered discreetly into my ear.

I wasn't so sure we could, so I stepped away from him, walked to the bar and poured myself a refill.

'Hey guys, having fun?' asked Charlie, who strutted towards us. I couldn't help but notice several men stare at her. She really was a bit of a sex kitten, especially dressed like that.

'Yes, absolutely. It's a fabulous party. Your house is beautiful. I noticed you gave Matt the grand tour earlier.'

She nodded. 'Yes, yes. Thank you. Adam, why don't you show Eve the rest of the house while I go and be the hostess with the mostess?'

This time it was Adam's turn to redden, and he looked away.

'Well? What are you waiting for?'

I reluctantly smiled and nodded.

'Okay then, Eve. Follow me,' he said.

'Well, you've pretty much seen downstairs, why don't I show you upstairs?' he said, through gritted teeth.

'You really don't have to, you know?'

'Charlie and Matt both want me to give you the tour, so I'm giving you the tour,' he said. 'Let's just act normally and walk up the stairs,' he added quietly.

The wine was going to my head, so I just nodded and followed him, looking down at the party below. Everyone was in good spirits, and I noticed that more people were dancing now. Even Matt and Charlie had got up and were strutting their stuff to Kylie Minogue's Spinning Around.

Adam stopped ahead of me and looked down to see what I was looking at. 'Looks like they're having fun,' he said. 'Charlie rarely dances with me. She doesn't like the way I do it.'

'No? That's a shame. I love dancing.'

'Oh, really? Anyway, follow me.'

I continued to walk behind him until we reached the second floor, where he showed me the two large spare bedrooms, which shared a bathroom.

'Beautiful bathroom,' I whispered, as I walked in and admired the floor to ceiling mosaic tiles and walk-in shower with separate bathtub.

'It is quite special, but it hasn't been used very much. Maybe when the kids come to stay.'

'Oh, I'd forgotten about your kids. How are they getting on at uni?'

He smiled proudly as he talked about them. It was nice. 'They're doing great, but Jack's not at university any more. He graduated last year.'

'Jack? I don't think you ever told me their names.'

'No? My eldest is Jack, and my youngest is Amy.'

'Lovely,' I said, as I sat on the edge of the bath and looked out the window. 'Wow, what a great view from here. I think you've got the best view on the street. We can't see the countryside like this. It's stunning.'

'We were lucky to find this house, I guess.'

'Yes, I suppose so. So tell me about Jack. What is he doing now that he's finished his studies?'

He smiled again and leaned against the doorframe. 'He studied architecture and was lucky enough to get a work placement in quite a sought after office in Bristol.'

'You sound very proud.'

'I am.' He grinned, taking a sip of his wine.

'And Amy?'

'Amy is studying at Bournemouth to become an interior designer.'

'Wow, that's impressive. Did she have anything to do with the design of this place?'

'As a matter of fact, she did. Charlie wasn't too thrilled about it, though.'

'Really? Why not? Don't they get on?'

'Not terribly well. Amy doesn't quite approve of my choice of wife.'

'Oh, dear.'

'Tell me about it. Shall we continue?'

'Yes please,' I said, standing and taking one more glance out at the spectacular view beyond the houses.

'These lead up to the master suite,' he said, standing to one side and letting me climb the stairs in front of him. I tried not to think of his eyes on me, but I knew he was looking at every curve of my body.

As we reached the top, there was a cosy lounge. I stepped aside so he could lead the way.

'Here's the bedroom,' he breathed as I followed him into a large room where one wall was painted black and the rest cream. Bright pink chairs with golden scatter cushions stood in either corner of the room, and a large four-poster dominated the space. Animal print rugs were carefully placed over the top of a cream shag pile carpet. Somehow the room didn't quite match the rest of the house. My opinion clearly showed on my face, and Adam looked a little downtrodden.

'It's grim, isn't it?'

'Grim?' I asked, trying ever so hard not to laugh. 'I take it that Charlie was allowed to decorate this room.'

Adam nodded, and I let out a deep laugh. 'Oh dear, Adam. Now I understand why you had Amy do the rest.'

'I know. I've been trying to convince her to change it, but she's having none of it.'

'Well, you've only been here, what – a month? You've got plenty of time to work on her. I'm sure you can use your charming ways to convince her.' I smiled and leaned on the wall beside a large nude painting of a woman with large boobs.

'Is this... Charlie?' I asked.

Again, Adam frowned before nodding. 'I'm afraid so.'

'Did you paint it?' I asked, stepping back to get a good look. I turned my head sideways, trying to work it out.

'Erm, no, I certainly didn't,' he laughed. 'It was by one of her gay best friends. Well, she told me he was gay. I never met him.'

I turned to look at him, and we both burst out laughing.

'It truly is horrendous.' I giggled. 'She's got very good boobs, though.'

'I prefer them somewhat smaller,' Adam whispered, and there was that familiar sensation again, rising up from my groin to my heart. I stepped towards the door.

'We should return to the party.' I smiled tightly. 'Before... well, just before...'

Adam stared at me for a moment before he grinned and followed me out the door.

CHAPTER 4

att stood in the bathroom doorway, staring at me. He was drunk. I could see that the whites of his eyes were bloodshot. I switched my bedside light off and turned over, but it wasn't enough. He climbed into bed and reached for me. I hated it when he was drunk. He fumbled around for a bit, while I lay on my back, looking up at the ceiling in the dark.

'C'mon baby, get in the mood,' he slurred.

'I am,' I whispered back.

'No, you're not, you're just lying there. Do something.'

I sighed and pushed him off me, climbing out of bed. 'You're drunk,' I said, as I walked into the bathroom and closed the door.

'Don't be silly. Come on, I want to have some sex.'

'Do it yourself, then,' I muttered, as I sat on the toilet and waited for him to go to sleep.

But it was no use, he was out of bed. I could hear his feet padding across the carpeted floor. He knocked on the door.

'Come on out, baby. I need you.'

'No, you don't,' I whispered. 'You just need a vessel to stick your dick into.'

I sighed and thought about earlier, standing in that hideous bedroom with Adam. Immediately, I began to throb between my legs. I stood up and opened the door.

Matt grinned and stumbled slightly, pulling me back to the bed.

I closed my eyes and straddled him as we sat on the edge. My mind wandered to the only person I wanted to be screwing, and he was next door, perhaps screwing his wife. God, this was totally messed up, I thought as I began to move faster and faster. Keeping my eyes closed, I pushed him backwards and readjusted myself on top of him for full effect. It didn't take long for me to reach orgasm. Matt was a little slower, so I tried to roll over with him on top, but he grabbed me roughly and turned me around, entering me from behind. This was why I didn't like it when he was drunk. He got a bit carried away, and sometimes it hurt. He wasn't doing it on purpose, I knew that, but still; I didn't like it.

Eventually, he started moving quicker and quicker until he shuddered and stopped.

'Tissue,' I whispered.

He leaned over and grabbed the toilet roll, handing it to me. I unravelled a bit to prevent the wet patch and hobbled back into the bathroom to clean myself up.

Matt was fast asleep when I went back to bed. He probably wouldn't even remember that we'd had sex when he woke up in the morning.

I lay there looking at him in the moonlight for a while. He was really handsome. He'd always made a real effort to have a good body, with his cycling and the gym he used almost every day. Sometimes he went swimming, too. A surfer as well - whenever he got the chance to go away, he'd go. And I'd use that time to write. We gave each other freedom, and that was important to both of us. He let out a sudden snort and turned his head, giving me a better profile view of his classic features. His nose was a little long, but it fit perfectly with the rest of his face. He had the deepest of blue eyes, not that I could see them. In fact, it was his eyes that had drawn me to him, all those years earlier. That and his dark red hair. His colour was unique, and so was he. That's what I'd thought at the time. We'd fallen in love almost instantly and were living together within four months.

I sighed and turned away, curling up into a ball. Where and when had it gone wrong? Was it Adam? Had I ruined it? A tear rolled down my cheek. Had I done this to us? Was I really to blame?

oOo

'Morning,' I said, as I stood checking the week's post as Matt walked into the kitchen, rubbing his eyes and yawning. I handed him a large cup of black coffee without him even having to ask for it. I just knew he needed it.

He took it and looked at me gratefully as he took a long drink. Sighing, he sat down at the breakfast bar.

'How are you feeling?' I asked.

He raised his eyebrows.

'You were quite drunk last night.'

He nodded. 'Yes, I think I must've been,' he said, rubbing his temples. 'I must have fallen asleep as soon as my head hit the pillow,' he muttered.

I didn't say anything about the rough sex. There wasn't any point. 'You danced a lot.' I smiled, remembering how happy he'd seemed.

'Did I?' He thought for a moment. 'Oh yeah, I suppose I did. It was a good night. Maybe we should throw a party soon, too.'

'A party? Whatever for?'

He shrugged. 'Just for the fun of it.'

'Maybe at Christmas,' I suggested.

'That's not exactly soon, though, is it?'

'A few months. It's enough.'

He shrugged. 'They've got a great house, haven't they?'

'Hm? Yes, they do. Beautiful.'

'Especially the master suite. I did like that.'

I burst out laughing, expecting him to laugh with me, but he just looked at me quizzically.

'What are you laughing at?'

'I thought you were being sarcastic.'

He slowly shook his head. 'No. I quite liked it.'

'Oh, Matt, it's hideous. That woman has no clue when it comes to interior decorating.'

'I just think it has... plenty of personality.'

'Yes, you could definitely say that,' I said, shaking my head. When had we become so different? We used to have the same style, the same ideas when it came to how to decorate our rooms. And now? Well, I'd much rather have Amy's assistance than Charlie's.

'I prefer the rest of their house, myself.'

Matt nodded, standing up to go and make himself a slice of toast. 'It lacks a little something if you ask me.'

'Really? You know it was Adam's daughter that did the rest?'

'I had no idea. I didn't even know he had a daughter.'

I nodded. 'Yes, Amy is at university in Bournemouth, studying to become an interior designer. He has a son, too; Jack.'

Matt barely acknowledged me while he stuffed his marmite-covered toast into his mouth, 'I'm going for a shower.'

'Okay. You going out after?'

'I think I made plans to do something. Can't quite put my finger on what, though. I'm sure a shower will help me remember.'

'Maybe. I just hope it's not anything particularly important.'

'No, probably not. Something I organised last night. It'll come to me soon enough.'

'Well, it's almost half past nine, so whatever it is, I hope it wasn't too early.'

He ignored me and walked up the stairs, and I returned my attention to the mail. Just bills, random leaflets and my magazine subscription. I tossed them onto the kitchen counter and went to the bottom of the stairs.

'I'm going to yoga,' I yelled. 'I'll see you later.'

'See you in a bit,' he shouted back before I heard the water come on in the shower.

oOo

'Oooh,' I groaned as I leaned forward, stretching my legs straight out in front of me. It was my least favourite yoga move, but it did wonders for my lower back. Spending so much time sitting at a desk at my computer meant my back often ached, but the yoga was helping tremendously. And I was thoroughly enjoying it. The group that attended were really good fun, and I'd frequently go for a cup of coffee with one or two of the ladies afterwards.

'And now the shoulder stand,' said Amelia, the yoga teacher, after we'd done a few other poses. I carefully threw my legs over my head until they were touching the floor. Breathing slowly for a few moments, I then lifted them upwards so that they were straight out above me. Amelia walked over and just pulled my legs up a little more. 'That's better, Eve. You weren't quite upright,' she said, walking over to the girl next to me.

After three minutes of being in the shoulder stand, we gently lowered our legs before we slowly sat up and continued with the other moves. Soon though, it was time for deep relaxation. A time to clear the mind and totally relax. I often found my mind drifting to whatever I was working on at the time, but lately, all I could think about was one thing. Or should I say one man?

CHAPTER 5

I always felt so good after my yoga workout, fully stretched, focussed and ready for the day. I always went to a class on Sunday, while the rest of the week I tried to do half an hour at home. Matt had tried it once with me but spent most of the time laughing because he kept farting. It was very distracting, so I was glad when he told me he didn't fancy doing it again. Thank God for that.

Climbing out of my little Fiat 500, I shut the door and walked into the house to be met by nothing but silence.

'I'm back, Matt. Are you home?' I listened for a moment, but nothing.

Dropping my handbag and yoga mat at the foot of the stairs while I took off my jacket, I hung it up before heading to the kitchen to get a glass of water. On the table was a hastily written note:

I REMEMBERED! I'd arranged to go for a cycle with Charlie. Tried to get Adam to come but he wasn't keen – no surprise there. See you later x

I SCRUNCHED IT UP, dropped it into the recycling bin and stood

37

gulping down a tall glass of water, before pouring a second. I let it slide down my throat, soothing my thirst, while I wondered what to do with my day. Opening the fridge, I decided I ought to go and get some groceries; otherwise Matt would complain about the lack of food later.

The supermarket was so crowded; it had been stupid to go on a Sunday morning. I should have done the shopping earlier in the week, I thought, as I waited in line for a parking spot, drumming my fingers on the dashboard to the sounds of Lady Antebellum's American Honey. A few months ago, this would have probably left me feeling impatient and stressed out, but yoga had undoubtedly helped calm me down. I smiled at the thought. My yoga teacher, Amelia, was a woman in her sixties who looked twenty years younger, even though she was completely natural, with long silky white hair. She was a real beauty, in and out. The sort of person I'd like to become.

Not likely, said the devil on my shoulder. Not with you screwing up your marriage. Lusting after another woman's husband. I bet Amelia wouldn't do such a thing.

I sighed and finally turned into a parking space, narrowly missing a man who had rushed across right in front of me. Idiot. Breathe, Eve, breathe. Think of yoga. Don't think of betrayal and infidelity.

Betrayal. Infidelity. In some cultures, I'd be stoned to death. I shuddered. It was only once. Well, not counting the kiss last night. The kiss. I'd almost forgotten about it. How could I?

Because you're trying to force it from your subconscious, repeated the devil. Don't bother. You did it. You kissed him. He kissed you. What's wrong with that?

Everything, said the angel. You're a married woman, Eve. You don't need anyone else. You need to make it work with Matt. Maybe you should move house.

Move house? I almost crashed my trolley into a stressed young woman with three children. I smiled apologetically, and she returned the gesture.

Maybe I should think about moving house. Perhaps I'd bring it up with Matt later.

'Why do you want to move house?'

'Because I slept with the neighbour.'

Yeah, that would go down well, wouldn't it?

Totally distracted, I failed to notice that a young child to my right had been trying to pull a tin of beans out from the bottom of a pyramid of cans. Before I could realise what was happening, there was a loud crash, and they all came falling down, some of them right on top of me. I dodged most of them but couldn't help some of them from crashing into my shin and foot.

I yelled and stumbled, just catching myself from falling to the ground over the tins, which were now scattered and rolling all over the supermarket floor.

Several employees came rushing over while the child sat crying in the corner. Fortunately, he'd had the sense to get away before receiving any injuries. Mortified, his mother grabbed him and screamed at him. She'd clearly seen everything happen.

'Are you alright, madam?' said a helpful young man wearing the supermarket's logo on his apron.

'Yes, I think so,' I said, hobbling a little. 'Just a sore foot, I reckon. Don't worry, I'll be fine.'

'I'm so sorry,' said the child's mother. 'Are you sure you're okay?'

I nodded and smiled. 'It was an accident,' I said, glancing at the child, who looked up surprised. 'He didn't do it on purpose.'

'I won't do it again,' he said, tears pouring down his cheeks.

'Say sorry to the lady,' his mother urged.

The little boy tucked his face into his mother's shoulder and cried.

'Samuel, say sorry.'

He slowly turned his head back, so he was looking at me. I waited patiently. 'I'm sorry,' he half-whispered and half-cried.

'You're forgiven,' I said, ruffling his hair.

'Thank you,' his mother said, as she walked back to her trolley and placed him in it before she turned back to me with a smile. She continued to the checkout, no doubt trying to get out as fast as possible.

'What happened here?' said the store manager who waddled into view. She was small and round, with a face that was both angry and sympathetic at the same time. 'I specifically requested that the cans not be stacked in such a way, and yet, continuously, my orders are not followed. And now look what's happened. Was anyone hurt?' she demanded of her staff, who were busy trying to collect the rolling cans.

'That lady over there.' The young man who had appeared first on the scene pointed at me.

She waddled over, looking very worried that I might sue or something. She glanced down at my legs and winced. 'Goodness me,' she sighed. 'You're bleeding. Please come with me so we can clean you up.'

'Oh, there's really no need. I'll be fine. I'll just carry on with my shopping. As I turned to walk away though, my foot seemed to give way, and I winced in pain. 'Oh,' I cried. 'Perhaps it's worse than I thought.'

'Eve?' said a voice from the adjoining aisle.

Looking up, I noticed Adam carrying an empty shopping basket, walking briskly towards me. 'Whatever happened to you?'

I laughed and winced at the same time. 'Just had a little accident with some baked beans.'

With raised eyebrows, he looked down at my leg. 'Ouch,' he said and turned to the store manager. 'Leave it to me,' he said and handed his basket to her before he bent down and picked me up as if I weighed nothing.

'Oh Adam, there's really no need. I'm fine,' I cried.

'Nonsense. Right, is there somewhere we can clean her up?'

The round woman nodded and suggested we follow her, where we walked through a door off limits to the general public and ended up in a large room with a few tables and chairs and a small sofa in the corner.

After she'd rallied around me and cleaned up my wound, putting a large plaster over it with a silly grin, she said, 'Now I'd usually be giving you a lollipop, but I think you've probably grown out of them.'

We all laughed as I shook my head. 'I don't know. Whoever grows out of sucking on a lollipop?'

She pretended to go and get one, and I shook my head. 'No, no, I was joking.'

When the laughter had subsided, Adam looked at me and leaned forward. 'Right, we should get you home.'

'No, I'm fine. I can walk, I'm sure. I need to finish my shopping first.'

'Well, I'm going to help you then. Thank you for your help with my... friend here,' he said to the store manager, who smiled back.

'No problem. I'm just very sorry that it happened. I will be looking into who stacked the beans in such a stupid way, and they will be reprimanded.'

'Oh, please don't. It's a mistake that anyone could have made. I'm really alright. There's no need.'

'Well, if you're sure?' she said.

'I am, honestly.'

'Okay then,' she smiled. 'Let me show you the way back to the store.'

Back in the central part of the supermarket, I hobbled, ungracefully leaning on Adam while we finished getting the remainder on my shopping list. He insisted that he do everything while I rested my leg, and once it was all paid for and packed in the boot of my Fiat, he turned and smiled at me.

'Well, the least I can do is buy you a cup of coffee,' I offered, looking towards the Starbucks just across the road in the retail park.

'That sounds like a plan,' he said. Before I had a chance to react, I was in his arms again. I laughed as he carefully waited for a couple of cars to pass before striding across the road and very gently putting me down in front of the large welcoming doors of my favourite coffee shop. A man with a newspaper was just standing up to leave as we entered, so we carefully made our way over to his table. Adam made sure I was comfortable before returning to make the order.

I sighed and looked out the window. What a morning. I spotted the woman with the young boy who'd caused quite a stir. She looked ever so stressed out, but she still smiled when she noticed me looking at her. She nodded and gave me the thumbs up. 'Still okay?' she mouthed.

I smiled and nodded, returning the thumbs up.

Grinning, she looked in her mirror and then pulled out of the parking space. She waved to me and was gone.

'Friend of yours?' asked Adam as he placed two large identical frothy coffees on the table.

'Ooh wonderful, thank you. Er, no, not really. It was her little boy who knocked the beans over.' I laughed.

'Oh,' he laughed. 'Little monster.'

'Quite. Actually, he was a little sweetie. All kids like to experiment, really, don't they?'

'Yes, they certainly do. My Jack was a little nightmare. His terrible twos lasted well into his threes and fours.' He chuckled. 'But he grew out of it, thankfully. Probably didn't help that his mother used to spoil him rotten. Did you never want children?'

'Yes, absolutely, but I had some serious issues and had to have a hysterectomy in my late twenties,' I said, stirring my coffee. It had taken a long time, but I'd finally come to terms with my lack of childbearing abilities.

'Jesus, Eve. I'm so sorry.'

'Thanks, but I'm okay about it now. I've accepted that Matt and I weren't meant to be parents. It was tough for a while, but we got through it.'

Adam nodded. 'I have lots of childless friends who are very happy. They had more money and time to devote to themselves, some of them have a lot more holidays than those of us with kids.'

'Yes, I can imagine,' I replied. 'We've had some fabulous holidays that we wouldn't have been able to afford if we'd had children.'

'Yes, you told us about Vegas and New York. Such a coincidence that we were there at the same time.'

'It's a small world,' I said, taking a sip of my ginger spice soy latte.

'Erm, you've got a bit of a...' he leaned over slightly and wiped my lip with his finger. '...a milk moustache.'

Blushing intensely, I sat back in my chair and laughed. His

touch had zapped me again, and I needed a moment to try and calm down.

'You feel it too, don't you?' he whispered.

I looked up and nodded.

'Jesus, it's like an electrical jolt or something. I've never experienced it before,' he said with a smile.

'I have.'

'Oh?' He looked disappointed.

'In London, about three years ago,' I said, trying not to smile but failing miserably.

His grin lit up his face. I just sat looking at him for a moment. He was so different from Matt, with his short black hair and eyes that were such a dark shade of brown that they could almost be described as black. He had a flatter nose than my husband, and his skin was a deep shade like he'd spent months in the sun, though it was just his natural colour. He had quite high cheekbones. He was just so beautiful.

'What?' he eventually asked. 'What are you looking at? What are you thinking?'

I looked away and took another sip of coffee, careful to avoid the milk moustache this time.

'Tell me.'

I shrugged. 'I was just thinking about how different you are from Matt.'

'Oh, yes. I guess so. Very different, in fact.' He smiled.

'And how different I am from Charlie.'

'In every possible way.' His smile widened. 'Especially your ability to decorate your home.'

I laughed and threw back my head. 'You know Matt really likes your master bedroom?'

Adam flared his nostrils and laughed loudly, causing the people at the next table to stare. 'Oh, dear. Well, what can I say?'

'Not a lot, really.' I chuckled. 'You know they're cycling together this morning?'

'Yes, Charlie asked me to go too, but she knew I wouldn't. I'm not a cycler.'

'You mean a cyclist?' I joked.

'That too.' He winked.

'It seems they have more in common than they do with you and me,' I sighed.

'I know, weird right?'

I nodded.

'I was actually thinking of moving, this morning,' I admitted.

'Moving? You mean moving house? Why would you want to do that?'

I shrugged my shoulders and looked at him. 'Isn't it obvious?'

'Oh, I suppose it is. But there's no need to do that. I'm sure we can resist each other, can't we?'

I could practically hear my heart thudding in my chest, and the hairs on the back of my neck stood on end just thinking about him in that way. 'I...I don't know, Adam,' I whispered before I stood up quickly. 'I think I should go now. Thank you for the coffee, even though it was supposed to be my treat.'

'Oh, yes, of course. My pleasure.'

I had forgotten about my painful leg, of course, and when I turned to walk out, it hit me, and I felt a little sick. 'Oh,' I uttered under my breath.

'Are you alright?' he asked, rushing to my side and taking my weight.

'Who'd have known a few cans of beans could cause such pain,' I said, trying to smile. 'Just help me to my car please, Adam.'

He nodded and carefully took my arm. 'Lean on me as much as you can,' he whispered as we walked between the tables and out into the fresh air. Then he lifted me up into his arms again and walked back to my car.

'I'm not sure you should drive like this, Eve. Let me drive you home?'

'No, I can drive. I'm sure I can. Let me try.'

He nodded and took the key from my hand, unlocking and opening the car, and I slowly placed myself into the seat. But when I turned and put my foot on the clutch, pain shot up my leg, and I let out a little yelp.

'No, you'll have to come with me,' he insisted. 'Wait here, and I'll and bring my car over. We can put your groceries into my boot and Adam can come and pick your car up later. I presume he's insured to drive it?'

I nodded.

'I'll be right back. Stay here.'

I nodded again and waited while he walked away towards his black BMW. Moments later, he pulled up beside me and transferred all my shopping bags into his car before he turned his attention back to me. He was such a gentleman as he opened the door and helped me, putting the seat back as far as possible so I could keep my leg straight out in front of me.

'Thank you, Adam. I do feel like a moron, though.'

He smiled at me sideways as we drove out into the traffic. 'It could have happened to anyone.'

'Yes, but it happened to me. I'm an idiot.'

'Don't be silly.'

I shrugged and relaxed into the seat. I didn't want to go home. I didn't want to think about anyone else. I just wanted to be with him. But it was impossible; I had to go home. I had to unpack my groceries, and I had to think about dinner for Matt and me. Not dinner for me and Adam. I sighed heavily.

'What's up?'

'Nothing,' I offered. 'Everything. Life.'

'Is it that bad?'

I turned to look at him as he concentrated on the red light ahead of us. 'No, of course not. I have a good life with Matt. We've been together for a long time. We always used to say we were soul mates.'

'Used to?'

'Sorry?' I said.

'You said used to say you were soul mates.'

'Did I?' I hadn't even realised. When was the last time we'd really told each other that we loved each other? Not the everyday words that had become a habit, but the profound, meaningful words meant for two people so desperately in love that they can barely let each other out of sight? A year? Two? Three? Maybe even longer.

'Maybe you've both grown apart?' he whispered, pulling the car into the driveway.

I ignored his suggestion and answered with my own question. 'I wonder if they're home yet?'

The garage door was closed, and there was no sign of them anywhere.

'It must be a long cycle route,' Adam said.

As I rifled around in my handbag, I picked up my mobile and looked at the screen.

'There's a message,' I said. 'Got side-tracked. Cycled for miles. A bit tired, so we're stopping for lunch. Be home late this pm. Luv x'

'Well, it looks like it's just you and me.' Adam smiled as he helped me out of the car.

I hobbled over to the front door.

'Wait, don't walk. I'll carry you,' he offered.

'No need. I'm here already,' I said, putting the key into the lock.

'Well, at least let me make sure you get to a chair safely,' he said, picking me up again and carrying me over the threshold.

'Oh Adam, I'm fine,' I said, as he carried me into the living room and placed me on the chaise-longue, my favourite piece of furniture. He very carefully lifted my leg up and untied the laces on my trainer, slowly pulling it off my swollen foot. I winced as he removed the sock like a surgeon.

'Oh Eve, it's black and blue. Keep it elevated for a bit. I'll go and get everything out of the car. Can I get you a drink first?'

I shook my head. 'No, I'll be okay. Just... just... come back quickly,' I said, looking at him intensely. He kissed me on the forehead and smiled.

'I'll be right back, I promise.'

CHAPTER 6

I must have dozed off, because when I woke up, Adam was sitting beside me, my foot resting carefully on his thigh as he wrapped it in a wet bandage.

'Oh, did I fall asleep?'

He smiled and nodded. 'Not for long, though, don't worry. Only about twenty minutes.'

'What's that smell?' I asked, looking at the bandaged foot.

'Witch hazel. It's good for drawing out the bruise.'

'Really? How do you know all this stuff?'

'My ex-wife was into it.'

'Gosh, you have a good memory.'

'Actually, I don't. I called her.'

I smiled before blushing. 'What did you tell her?'

'That a very good friend of mine had been in an accident and ended up with a badly bruised foot and a bloody leg.'

I groaned. 'Thank you for not including the baked beans.'

'Well actually, now that you mention it...' He laughed.

I smacked my forehead.

'She was amused but concerned. She wanted to come and tend to you herself.'

'Really?'

Adam nodded. 'But perhaps that's more because she wants to meet you.'

47

'She wants to meet me? Why on Earth would she want to meet me?' I waited for a moment, my imagination going wild. 'Oh Adam, she knows, doesn't she?'

He looked away, embarrassed.

'How could you? How could you tell anyone?' I tried to remove my foot from his thigh, but he held my leg firmly, not letting me go.

'Please don't be upset,' he replied, 'it was after London. Before the wedding. She knew something was wrong, and she kept on insisting I tell her, so I did.'

'But you told her about me here, now?'

'She knew. She said it was my voice. It gave me away.'

'Let's hope that your current wife isn't as perceptive as your ex-wife,' I said bitterly.

'Please, Eve. Don't be like that. Lisa is different. I've always confided in her. She's a friend. Don't worry about her. She won't tell a soul, I promise you that.'

I closed my eyes and breathed loudly.

'I'm sorry to have upset you. Would you like me to leave?' he asked.

My eyes shot open, and I shook my head. 'No, I don't want you to leave... And therein lies the problem,' I added with another sigh.

With the bandage firmly in place, Adam began to make circles on my ankle with his thumb. The slightest touch had such a massive effect, and I felt like I might explode.

'A-A-Adam. Don't.'

'I can't help it, Eve. I want to touch you all the time. Every minute of every day.'

'I know.'

Slowly he scooted forward so that my legs were straddling him. He leaned over and kissed my neck, upwards towards my ear, cheek and then he pecked the tip of my nose. I closed my eyes and groaned. He kissed my left eye and then my right, then back down, kissing my cupid's bow before he opened his mouth and pushed mine open with his tongue. It was delicious. I throbbed every-where, from the soles of my feet up to my knees – up, up, up – and bang between my legs. Like a firework had gone off inside me.

'Oh Adam,' I groaned. 'I want you so much.'

His hands moved carefully over my shoulders and down each arm, circling, probing, across to my breasts, which were aching to be touched. He slid his hand down my top, carefully moving my bra to one side so he could trace my nipple.

I was on fire, and no amount of water could put me out.

That is until there was a knock at the door.

'Shit,' I exclaimed, pushing myself off him guiltily.

Adam swallowed loudly and sat back, closing his eyes, trying to contain himself and calm down the massive erection bulging in his trousers.

I rearranged my bra and brushed myself down, using my hands to flatten my hair.

'I'd better get it,' he said. 'You shouldn't walk.'

'Ahem,' I said, pointing to the continued bulge.

'Oh, I'm trying to...'

'I'll go. It is my house, after all.'

Stumbling clumsily across the living room, I closed the interior door behind me and leaned back against it. Taking a deep breath, I hobbled to the front door.

Opening it, I was shocked to find my parents standing on the step.

CHAPTER 7

'*S*urprise!' they yelled together.

'Mum, Dad. What on Earth are you doing here? I didn't know you were in England? This is a surprise.'

'Well, come on then, love, let us in. We're dying for a cuppa.'

'Of course. Come on in. Go right through to the kitchen. I'll be right there.'

Mum and Dad waltzed in and headed straight for the living room.

'No!' I yelled.

'What? What's up, love?'

'It's much more comfortable in the kitchen,' I said, sounding ridiculous.

'Since when?' Mum replied, turning the handle.

'I found it,' called a strangled voice from the kitchen, and Adam walked into the hallway carrying another bandage. 'What are you doing on your feet? The nurse said to stay horizontal,' he admonished innocently.

'Oh, who's this?' asked my dad, as he looked at Adam, then the bandage, then me and then my foot.

'Oh, for Heaven's sake, love, whatever have you done to your foot?'

'It's nothing, Dad. Nothing to worry about.'

'Nonsense,' said Adam, as he approached me and forced me to

lean on him as he helped me back into the living room, where he placed me back on the chaise-longue.

'I'm Adam, by the way,' he said, straightening up and walking over to my parents and shaking their hands. 'I live next door. I bumped into Eve in the supermarket earlier, just after she'd had a bit of a run-in with a few tins of baked beans.' He smiled, returning to sit beside me where he started pretending to re-bandage my foot.

'Oh, hello, dear, nice to meet you. Whatever happened with baked beans to result in that?' Mum pointed.

'Just some collapsed tins, that's all, Mum. There's no need to make a fuss. Adam was kind enough to drive me home and help bandage me up.'

'Her foot's black and blue underneath all this,' he added.

'Shouldn't we take you to the hospital?' Dad asked, intrigued by the bizarre set of circumstances.

'And where is Matt? Shouldn't he be here taking care of you?' Mum asked, clearly displeased with my husband. She'd always quite liked Matt, but she'd never really wanted to call him her 'son'.

'He's out cycling like he does most Sundays, Mum. Don't you remember?'

'Are you single, Adam?' she asked, as I pursed my lips to try and prevent myself from laughing.

'Erm, no. My wife, Charlie... Well, she's actually out cycling with Matt.'

Mum raised her eyebrows and pulled a knowing face rather like Hyacinth Bucket from that old TV show, Keeping Up Appearances, before looking at Matt and then at me.

'Your husband,' she pointed to me, before pointing at Adam, 'is out cycling with your wife?' she asked, now looking like she'd bitten into a whole lemon. An unripe one.

Both of us nodded slowly, glancing at each other like a couple of naughty school children.

'As long as it's only bikes they're riding,' Mum said.

'Mother!'

My dad was keeping quiet. Clearly, he was quite amused by the whole thing.

'Well, I suppose I'd better go and make us a cup of tea,' she said, standing.

'No, please let me do it... Mrs... Oh, I'm sorry, I don't know what to call you?' Adam asked, standing up.

'I'm Mrs Baggin,' Mum said, in a voice that was more like the Queen's than her real one.

'Oh, Mum, honestly. Joyce and George, Adam.'

'I'll make the tea, Mr and Mrs Baggin. I'll be right back.'

'But you don't know where everything is,' I cried, as he disappeared out of the room.

'I'll find it, don't worry,' he yelled back.

'So how long has it been going on?' Mum asked innocently.

'What? What do you mean?' I asked, feeling my face flush slightly.

'You and Adam? How long have you been sleeping together?'

My eyes rounded in shock. Mum and I have never had a conversation about sex, or anything like that, especially not in front of my dad. 'Don't be ridiculous, Mum. I'm married to Matt.'

She narrowed her eyes and stared at me for a second. 'If you say so.'

'I do,' I snivelled, feeling like a teenager again, not a thirty-nine-year-old grown woman.

'Take no notice of her, love. It's been a long day. She's just tired, that's all. How are you? How are the book sales going? Is Matt busy? What have you been up to?'

I laughed at my dad. 'Slow down, Dad! All in good time. I'm fine, thank you. I'm in the middle of writing my next book at the moment, and sales are going steady. I'd like it to be a bit – well, a lot – more, really, but one day it'll happen. I'm convinced I'll become a household name one of these days.' I grinned.

'That's my girl,' Dad replied. 'And Matt?' he asked tentatively. 'He been keeping busy?'

I nodded. 'Very.'

'Well, that is good to hear,' Mum interrupted. 'So, tell me more about Adam – your... next-door neighbour,' she emphasized.

I smiled at her and leaned back into the chair, readjusting my foot, as it was beginning to throb a little. 'Adam moved in next door just over a month ago, and we've become friends. He's a very nice man, and his wife is lovely too,' I added for effect.

'And children? Do they have any children?'

'I have a son and a daughter,' Adam replied for me, as he pushed open the door and set the tray on the coffee table. In the middle sat a teapot – one that was a wedding gift, and had probably never been used, and some posh cups and saucers that were only used on special occasions. Clearly, Adam knew how to make my mum feel special. I grinned at him as he proceeded to pour tea for us all.

'Thank you, dear,' Mum said. 'So, tell me about your children. I do like to hear about people's children.'

I looked down at the floor. She'd been devastated after my hysterectomy. Being an only child meant she'd never have any grandchildren of her own, and that was like the end of the world to her. I don't think she'd ever quite forgiven me for having all my bits and pieces removed, even though she knew it was necessary. I could have died, otherwise, and she understood that. But deep down, she needed to blame someone, and it had to be me. And I understood that.

When I lifted my head, having zoned out for a bit, Dad was looking at me like his heart was broken. I smiled as he tipped his head and blew me a kiss. He always used to do that when I was a kid, and it never failed to make me laugh. I pretended to catch the kiss, just as I had done over thirty years ago. Dad winked at me before I heard Mum ask Adam even more personal questions.

'Mum, give the guy a rest, already. Sorry, Adam. She does like to pry.'

Adam looked across at me and smiled, 'It's fine. I don't mind.' He grinned at her, and she blew her chest up like a cockerel. Was it a cockerel that did that? Anyway, she was clearly falling a bit in love with Adam. I knew the moment he'd talked about children, it would change her opinion of him. And the second he'd mentioned that one day he'd like to be a grandfather... Well, if she could swoon, she would have swooned. It was embarrassing.

'Well, it's just a shame that you two aren't together, that's all I'm saying on the subject,' she said, pursing her lips together.

'No-one asked you, Joyce,' said my dad, finally, having had

enough of her ridiculous comments. 'Just leave the poor kids alone. They're friends.' He turned to face Adam. 'Adam, I'm grateful that my daughter has such a good friend to look after her at times like these. Those blessed baked beans.'

I couldn't help it. I burst out laughing. Adam looked at me and followed suit, and then my dad cracked up. My mum looked at us all. She tried not to – I could almost feel the strain in her chest – but even she saw the funny side, and soon the laughter was echoing throughout the house.

CHAPTER 8

'I'm sorry I missed your mum and dad, babe,' Matt said at the dinner table, later that night.

I smiled, pushing the pasta around my plate. 'That's okay. I don't think you're really sorry though, are you?'

'Well, you know your mum. She doesn't like me very much.'

'Yes she does,' I said, somewhat non-committal.

Matt raised his eyebrows. 'She hates me,' he said, putting the iPad down for a moment to take another mouthful of the bolognese.

'She so doesn't hate you. Okay, she doesn't love you, but she likes you.'

'She puts up with me because I'm your husband.'

'Well, if you put it that way, I suppose you're right.'

'How long are they in England?'

'Just a few days, Mum has one of her annual doctor's appointments. Just a check-up. Nothing to worry about.'

'Where are they staying this time?'

'Auntie Jean's.'

He nodded. 'How's your foot?'

'Better.'

'I still can't believe you got such a nasty injury from baked beans.' He laughed, almost spitting out the spaghetti that was hanging from his mouth. He sucked it back in with a loud, smacking sound, and I shook my head.

'You're so gross.'

'Maybe.' He grinned.

'Did Charlie enjoy the ride?'

Matt spat out the next mouthful as he coughed. 'Yes, yes, very much. We're going to do it again next weekend. Maybe you'd like to come along?' he suggested, looking eagerly at me.

I shrugged. 'It's a nice idea, but I wouldn't be able to keep up. You're both a lot fitter than me. I'd hate to be stuck miles behind. Plus, my foot.' I pointed to the bandaged appendage sticking up from where it was propped on the chair in front of me.

'Well, maybe we can convince Adam to come too. He's not very fit either, is he?'

'Oh, he's fit,' I said, trying not to smile. 'Just not on a bicycle.'

'Oh, does he go to the gym?'

'No, but he does a lot of gardening work.'

'Of course, yes. I'd forgotten about that. What's it called?'

'What?'

'His business?'

'Eden Grove Gardens.'

'He owns Eden Grove Gardens?'

I nodded. 'You sound surprised.'

'I am. Do you have any idea how big that is? He must be worth a fortune.'

'What do you mean?'

'They have garden centres all over the country. The landscape gardening must be just a sideline.'

'Oh, really? I had no idea. He doesn't seem the sort of person who'd be loaded, does he?'

Matt shook his head. 'No, not really.'

I played with my pasta a bit more and took a swig of water before pushing the dish away from me.

'Aren't you going to eat that?' he asked.

I shook my head. 'I'm not very hungry.'

Matt practically pounced on my leftovers, and all I could see was a caveman beside me, stuffing the food into his mouth, making all kinds of horrible sounds. I turned away. Why was he becoming more unattractive by the day? But I guess I knew the answer to that.

Stop it. He's your husband, and you love him, said the angel on my shoulder. He hasn't changed. Just love him. Be the wife you always wanted to be. Love him, care for him, be there for him.

'Will you pass me a lager, love?' he asked, burping.

'Would you mind getting it yourself? It's just that my foot is throbbing.'

'Oh yeah, forgot about that. Sorry.' He smiled and patted me on the head as he stood and walked to the fridge.

See, he's not so bad.

Closing the fridge door, he let out the biggest fart, which was followed by a horrible odour that drifted towards me before it engulfed me with all its powerful disgustingness.

'Eww, Matt. So gross,' I said, pulling my sweatshirt up so that it covered my nose and mouth.

He stood proudly with his hand on his stomach. 'Better out than in, right?'

'Yeah, I suppose so,' I grumbled.

A few years ago, I would've probably been rolling about on the floor laughing with him. How things had changed.

'Are you coming in to watch some TV?' he asked, as he stood by the door.

'Can you help me with the dishes first?'

'Oh yeah. Why don't you go and sit down, and I'll handle it?'

'Really?' I asked gratefully.

'Course,' he said. 'Here. Let me carry you into the lounge.'

I grinned at him and pushed my chair away from the table, carefully standing. He very gently leaned forward and put me over his shoulder in a fireman's lift.

Not quite what I had in mind, but it's the thought that counts, right?

He narrowly missed bashing my leg into the doorway in both the kitchen and the living room before plonking me down on the two-seat sofa. 'There,' he said, quite proud of himself. 'Okay?'

I nodded. 'I guess so. Thanks.'

'Do you want anything? A glass of wine? Cup of tea? Coffee? Baileys?'

'A glass of wine would be nice, thanks, darling.'

Matt winked at me, and he walked into the hallway just as the phone rang. 'I'll get it,' he yelled, a little louder than was necessary.

'Hey you,' I heard him say before he leaned back into the living room. 'I'll close the door, so I don't disturb your TV,' he said with a sheepish grin.

'Thanks, babe.'

'...had fun too...' I just about heard him say as he padded back into the kitchen.

Flicking through the channels, I settled on Strictly Come Dancing. I loved to watch the dancers strut their stuff; they were almost magical in their sequinned gowns, and the way they glided across the dance floor just took my breath away. I dreamed of being able to dance that way. I had been a good little dancer when I was young, but I rarely got the chance to do it these days. Matt didn't often dance with me. I'd suggested going to classes – Salsa or ballroom – but he didn't need to answer. His face answered for him. No way. Not in a million years.

I sighed as I watched them twirl and dip to the sounds of Meatloaf. A strange song choice, but they made it work. They were amazing. I almost wanted to clap and cheer them on.

I was so engrossed in the show that I'd almost forgotten about my wine. So in between dances, I decided to go and pour one myself.

I struggled off the sofa and hobbled to the door, which I pushed open to see down the hallway where Matt was leaning against the kitchen worktop smiling, murmuring. When he spotted me, his smile dropped for a second before he remembered my wine.

He smacked his hand to his forehead and, still listening to the other person on the phone, he took a glass out of the cupboard and the wine from the fridge and carefully poured some for me.

He pointed for me to sit back down. 'I'll bring it in. You sit down,' he mouthed.

I smiled at his thoughtfulness and returned to the sofa just as the next dance was about to start.

Matt walked in, the phone glued to his ear and handed me the wine.

'Thanks. Everything okay?' I asked.

He covered the phone with his hand. 'Yes, yes, fine. It's just Howard, nothing important.'

Content all was well, I returned my attention to the show and sat back to enjoy the Paso Doble, being performed by a rather old fellow, a celebrity I had never seen before.

CHAPTER 9

My foot was almost back to normal, and the small gash on my shin had scabbed over nicely. It had been two weeks since the accident, and life had proceeded as generally as it could with Adam living right next door. I had seen little of him, on account of him having to head up north to deal with some business issues at a new garden centre he'd opened in Northumberland somewhere.

I'd been busy finishing off the first draft of my book and so had little time to do anything else. I was typing like crazy, it was extraordinary. I'd never quite been so inspired, and the words were just flowing out of me like some kind of crazy – well, some kind of crazy writer.

It was fun; I was having the most fun I'd ever had writing. I smiled as I sat back in my little office and watched the dark clouds roll in from a distance. I hoped we were going to have a storm. I loved storms, there was something magical about them... all the grumbling in the distance and the intensity of the lightning bolts or sheets. Wonderful.

Glancing down the street, I spotted a familiar car turn into our road, a black BMW. A smile spread across my lips, and I could barely keep myself from jumping up and running out of the house and down into his arms. But I did contain myself. Adam and I hadn't been in close physical contact since the near-miss with my mum and dad. We'd agreed that was the last time. We couldn't risk being caught. We were both trying hard for the sakes of our families. I didn't want to hurt Matt, and he didn't want to hurt Charlie.

So, I was forcing myself to be content dreaming about him, fantasizing about him and just seeing him whenever I could. Even just watching him walk down the street to go to the local shop made me smile. I just loved knowing he was safe and well and close by.

It was almost impossible to keep myself from him, but we'd agreed to try, and try we would.

It was a Thursday afternoon, and when Matt had returned from work, he'd been eager to go out for a cycle. I watched him disappear down the road half an hour earlier before Adam arrived back from his travels.

He was lifting out a small holdall from the back of the BMW when he looked up and saw me in the window. His face lit up, and he waved.

I waved back.

He held up his hand and indicated a drink.

I nodded, and he pointed to his watch and held up five fingers before pointing to his house.

I gave him the thumbs up.

I'd be happy to be in his presence, even if Charlie was there. At that moment, I just wanted to be close to him, so I rushed out of my office and headed into the bedroom where I quickly changed into my most flattering pair of skinny jeans and jade green sweater, the one that revealed one shoulder. I pulled on my Ugg boots and squirted a little Dior perfume on to my neck before putting on a little black eyeliner and mascara, and just a swish of lip balm. I tipped my head upside down and tousled my hair with my fingers before flipping it back. Looking in the mirror, I smiled. I didn't look too bad.

Running down the stairs, careful to avoid putting too much pressure on my left foot, I grabbed my keys and phone and ran outside with a smile as the rain started to pitter-patter against the roof. Thunder echoed in the distance.

Adam stood at the door.

'Hey.' He grinned at me. 'Come in before you get wet.'

'Thanks. How was your trip?'

'Great, thanks. The business is fully up and running now. I have a feeling that's going to be particularly fruitful.'

'Great, I'm pleased for you.'

'How's Charlie? Is she here?' I asked, looking behind him for familiar signs of his wife.

'Actually, she's not here. She's gone to visit her sister in Bristol. She's staying a couple of nights to help look after the baby.'

'Baby?' I asked.

He grinned. 'Yes, Charlie is officially an auntie, as of yesterday.'

'Oh, wow, that's wonderful. She must be delighted. Aren't you going to visit?'

'It was a little difficult, what with business and everything. Plus, her sister and I don't really get on too well.'

'Oh no, why not?'

'She thinks I'm too old for her big sister.'

'Really? But you're only seven years older.'

He raised his eyebrows. 'Seven years too old, apparently.'

'Oh well. Sorry.'

He chuckled. 'Don't be. It doesn't bother me. If people don't like me, they don't like me. There's nothing I can do about it.'

'Good for you, but I can't imagine anybody not liking you. You're so... likeable.' I grinned.

'Glass of wine?' he asked, as I followed him through into the kitchen.

'Ooh, yes, please.'

'How have you been? Got much writing done?'

I could feel myself light up. 'Yes. I've written loads. I seem to be on a roll. I don't know what it is, but for the past month, my writing has gone through the roof. It's amazing. I absolutely love it, more than ever before. It's becoming even more of a real passion.'

'I can see that. You really light up when you talk about it.'

'I can feel myself lighting up.' I grinned as I took the glass of Portuguese wine from his fingers.

'Monte Velho? How on earth did you manage to find this? I love it. It's one of my favourites. I always drink it when I visit

Mum and Dad.' My eyes lifted to find his as it dawned on me and I chuckled, 'You've been in touch with Mum, haven't you?'

He nodded. 'You don't miss anything, do you? Yes, we swapped email addresses when we met. She insisted we keep in touch.'

'That's sweet. But why?'

'I think that's obvious, don't you?'

I shook my head.

'She clearly wants me to woo you away from your husband.'

'Oh God, my mother, honestly.' I shook my head.

'Don't worry, she just wants the best for you, that's all.'

'And the best for her, too.'

'Perhaps.'

'So she wants us to both break up our marriages and get together?'

'I think so.'

I laughed and moved away from him.

'How is Matt?' he asked, as we sat at the kitchen table and watched the brewing storm in the distance, as large droplets of water fell into the water fountain in the garden.

'Probably very wet, right now,' I said.

'Cycling?'

I nodded. 'Not the best day for it, but, hey, this is England. Cyclists over here are used to it, I suppose.'

As if he knew we were talking about him, my phone rang. 'Matt? Are you okay? I'm watching a pretty serious storm brewing. You should really get home as quickly as possible. What? What happened? Are you alright? Any damage? Oh, okay. As long as you're safe. No, no. I can come and get you if you want? Okay, yeah that's probably a good idea. Tell Howard I said hi. Okay, see you tomorrow, then. Be careful. Yeah, you too. Bye.'

'Is he alright?' asked Adam, his eyebrows furrowed.

'He's fine. He cycled right into the storm and had a bit of an accident. He can't cycle back, and they're miles away, so he's going to stay overnight with Howard, as the best cycle repair place is actually pretty close to Howard's. So, I erm... guess we're alone tonight.'

Adam looked down at me with such a serious expression. He stretched his arm and stroked my cheek.

'Can we try and stick to our agreement, Adam?' I whispered. 'Can we just be together this evening as friends? Can we just hang out together?'

He smiled and nodded, but his hand stayed stroking my face. 'I'm sure we can...try.'

I turned away with a grin. 'Well, we're on our own. What shall we do? What do you like doing that you don't do very often?'

'What about you? What do you like doing that you rarely get to do?' he asked.

I perched on the edge of the sofa and thought about it for a few moments. 'Anything?'

'Anything,' he replied.

'Dancing in the rain.'

Adam smiled and walked over to me, removing the glass of wine from my fingers, placing it next to his on the table. He went to his iPod and flicked through some of the songs until he found what he wanted, then he opened the sliding doors to the garden and grabbed me by the hand.

'Come on,' he said, as we stepped out into the pouring rain.

I giggled as my hair immediately stuck to the side of my face, and I tried to listen to the music as it began to play via the surround sound system.

Gene Kelly's voice started singing, and I shrieked with delight.

Adam stepped towards me and grabbed me, deftly dipping me backwards as Singing in the Rain and raindrops filled my ears. Laughter erupted from my lips. I couldn't stop giggling; it felt so good to dance in the rain. I felt so free, and Adam surprised me with his dance skills. He could move – really move. I could easily see him on Strictly, and I told him so. Why Charlie didn't like the way he danced, I'd no idea.

He grinned, spinning me one way and then the next, while we both sang along to the lyrics. I felt like someone in a movie, and I'd never felt like that before.

When the song came to an end, we just stood looking at each other, soaked to the bone, waiting for the next song to start.

When it began, I laughed so much, it gave me hiccups. The BeeGees' Staying Alive made me want to dance like a disco diva, and we both got into the groove, not caring that the thunder was practically overhead.

Only when fork lightning began to brighten the sky, and I looked a little worried, did he twirl me and twirl me until we were back indoors.

He pulled the doors closed, not caring that the tiled floor was now covered in water.

Opening a cupboard in the hall, he pulled out two large towels, handing me one as he quickly removed his clothes and wrapped himself tightly inside his.

I looked at his naked chest, and my knees went weak, but I forced myself to stop, and so I nervously climbed out of my drenched clothes and wrapped myself up as well. As tightly as possible.

We stood looking at each other before laughter erupted.

'What now?' I asked. 'What do you like doing that you don't normally get the chance to do?'

'You know the answer to that question,' he smirked.

'But not that. Anything but that,' I whispered.

'I'm trying, Eve. I'm really trying.'

'Me too, Adam, and we have to keep trying, okay?'

After a while, he nodded and then grabbed my hand. 'Can you swim?' he asked.

'Of course. But where can we swim?'

He touched the side of his nose and pulled me towards a bedroom on the ground floor. Opening a wardrobe door, he found a couple of T-shirts and a couple of pairs of sweatpants.

'Put these on,' he said. 'We're going for a ride.'

I looked at him like he was mad but did as I was told.

Before long, we were in his car, driving further out into the countryside. After about fifteen minutes, we arrived at the most beautiful big manor house, with the most exquisite gardens.

'Adam, it's stunning. Did you... did you design this garden?'

He grinned. 'Yes.'

'Whose house is this?' I asked, as we drove right up to the front door and climbed out, rushing undercover. Adam had a bunch of keys, which he deftly looked through before he found the one he was searching for. Slotting it into the door, he unlocked it and gently pushed me inside, out of the cold rain.

He said nothing as I gazed up in awe at the beautiful old house. It was like something out of a magazine, with beams above and the most stunning antique furniture, old mixed with new. We walked through the huge hallway, down a long corridor and down some stairs, which led to a door that went back outdoors.

'Where are we going?' I whispered.

'It's a surprise,' he said, as he pulled me along under a large canopy covered in climbing plants. At the end was another door, which he opened with a different key.

Pushing the door open, I could smell it before I could see it. Chlorine. Adam stepped away from me for a few minutes, and I stood trying to readjust my eyes to the darkness.

'Adam, where are you? What are you doing?'

Suddenly, there was a faint glow as a few lights in the swimming pool came on. The sound of something moving within the water made me look towards it, and I saw Adam standing in the pool. A haze rose around him.

'Come on in, it's warm,' he promised.

I grinned and climbed out of the trousers he'd lent me before removing the T-shirt. I didn't care that I was completely naked. In fact, I felt liberated as I stepped down the steps to join him. He stood watching, admiring me, his eyes following my every move. When the water reached my chest, I immersed myself fully and swam beneath it until I reached him. Feeling for him, my fingers found his firm thighs before I followed them upwards, feeling the hardness of his bottom and the base of his spine.

I slowly lifted myself out of the water until I stood facing him. He placed his hands underneath my arms and lifted me, slowly, twirling me around and around. The water whirled around my thighs. I became dizzy with happiness.

'Oh, Adam,' I sighed. As he eventually put me down, his arms must have ached, for sure.

'Whose place is this?'

Adam swam towards the edge of the pool and leaned backwards before answering me. 'It's mine, Eve.'

'What? What do you mean, it's yours?'

'I inherited it from my grandmother about two months ago.'

'Oh Adam, I'm so sorry,' I said, swimming towards him.

He shook his head and smiled at me.

'What?' I asked.

'Most people would be so awed by the house and the garden that they wouldn't even think about my loss. That actually means a lot. Thank you.'

I smiled. 'Tell me about your grandmother?' I asked.

He grinned and began to tell me all about the woman he'd adored. His parents had died within a year of each other when he was just seven, and old Nana Grove had taken over the parental duties. She'd found it difficult at first, but soon they'd become close.

'Don't you have any brothers or sisters?'

'I had an older brother, but he died with my dad in the car accident.'

'Oh, I had no idea. That's horrendous.'

'My mum couldn't cope, and she took her own life less than a year later.'

'Shit, Adam.' I said, pulling him towards me. 'Nobody should have to go through such a tragedy.'

'You did. With your grandparents.'

'You remembered?'

'I remembered everything you told me then, Eve. They died in a plane crash when you were a teenager.'

I nodded. It wasn't something I liked talking about, but I think Adam had gone through something far worse. I felt closer to him for feeling like he could speak to me about it.

'We've both seen tragedy,' he said sadly. 'Which is why we should be happy.' He pulled me towards him, and I let him.

His kiss was deep and full of longing. I returned it with equal desperation before pulling back with a grin and pushing myself off the side of the pool with both my legs.

I saw his grin, and he followed me until we were in the centre, treading water and holding on to each other as if our lives depended on it.

We moved along until our feet touched the tiles beneath us and then further until I was leaning back on the steps, and he was lying over me. He stared down into my eyes and kissed me again and again, until I flipped him over and straddled him, pulling his chest towards me, rubbing my nipples against him. I could feel his hardness sitting between us both, and God did I want him. I moved my hand down and stroked him, gently at first, slowly increasing the intensity until he became breathless. Then I pulled away from him and swam back to the side of the pool, pulling myself out, perching on the side with a grin. His gaze followed me, and then he slowly followed until he stood in front of me. His face level with the part of me that throbbed the most. He moved his head forward and licked the inside of my thigh. Leaning back, I smiled and placed my hands on the back of his head as he slowly moved it towards where I needed him.

Suddenly a light came on and broke the moment.

'Dad!' yelled a voice I was unfamiliar with.

Shock hit me, and I dropped immediately into the warm water, looking around to see where the voice had come from.

Adam froze, pushing me behind him.

'Jack? What the hell?' Adam said, unable to utter anything else.

'Dad, what are you doing here? And erm... Charlie? That wasn't Charlie, was it?'

Adam slowly shook his head. 'Jack, please would you go back inside and get yourself a drink. We'll be right in,' he said, shame written all over his face.

Mortified, I waited for his son to close the door behind him before I rushed to the side of the pool and pulled myself out.

'Oh God, I knew this was a bad idea,' I muttered. 'Are there towels anywhere?'

'Yes, just over there,' Adam pointed. He was clearly in more shock than I was if that were at all possible.

I grabbed them both, wrapping one around myself and handing the other to Adam.

Quickly drying ourselves, we put Adam's clothes back on without saying a word.

Just as I was about to push open the door, Adam grabbed my hand and pulled me towards him and hugged me.

'I'm so sorry about this. I'd forgotten that the kids had keys. I never expected this to happen. Please forgive me.'

I looked up and slowly extricated myself from his grip. 'Adam, it's as much my fault as it is yours. This should never have happened. It won't happen again,' I said, as I stepped back and went to open the door.

'Eve,' he cried, stepping forward. 'Please just kiss me. If this is our last, I want... please. Kiss me.'

His request brought tears to my eyes, and I pressed my lips against his, our tongues intertwining with lust and more. But I slowly broke away and stepped backwards.

'I'll wait in the car. And then I'd like you to take me home, please.'

Adam nodded. I knew he was watching me walk away.

CHAPTER 10

The night of our Christmas party was finally upon us, and as much as I'd tried to put it off, Matt had continued to push me to keep it on. I'd relented. How could I explain the reasoning behind wanting to cancel it?

Thankfully Adam's son had kept quiet, but he was a boy of strong morals, and he had insisted his father remain faithful to his wife. Needless to say, Jack was more important to him than anybody, so he'd agreed. We'd spoken, albeit briefly. Meals out with Charlie and Matt had been a little strained, although we'd managed to avoid becoming the centre of attention. Me feigning migraines and Adam excusing himself early with work issues. It had worked well until then.

Hopefully, it would be easy enough to avoid each other for one more night of partying. Matt had invited as many of his friends as possible. I, on the other hand, didn't want to involve anyone so had left the invites to my husband.

I was to play the dutiful wife, so I did my hair exactly how Matt liked it – up in a loose ponytail with a few soft ringlets dropping to each side of my face. I also let him choose my outfit, so I was standing in front of the mirror wearing a short black dress and pink high heels. It was a little over the top for me, but it was what Matt liked, so I went along with it.

'You look beautiful,' he said, standing in the bedroom doorway, looking at me.

'You think?' I asked uncertainly.

'I don't think. I know. You ready? Guests should be arriving at any minute.'

I nodded and took his arm.

'Right this way, Mrs Brooke.'

I smiled as we walked down the stairs and into the kitchen together, where he let me go and started double-checking that all the food and drinks were where they should be.

'I'm sure everything's fine,' I said as the doorbell rang. 'Go and greet your guests.'

'Don't you mean our guests?' he asked before walking out of the room.

I turned the oven off and pulled out the last of the nibbles as I listened to the laughter in the hallway. Forcing a smile, I turned to find Charlie walking towards me, carrying a bottle of wine.

'You look amazing, Charlie,' I said, kissing her on both cheeks.

Her dress was different from the style she usually wore, very floaty, with tonnes of fabric. She looked beautiful though, with her trademark bouffant hairdo.

Matt and Adam were shaking hands and exchanging the usual pleasantries as Charlie giggled. 'Can I pop to the loo?'

'Of course. You know where it is,' I said, watching her wiggle to the downstairs bathroom as the doorbell rang again.

Matt immediately headed to open it, and I stood in the kitchen with Adam.

'How are you, Adam?' I asked, pouring myself my first glass of wine. I knew it would probably be the first of many.

'Okay, I think. How are you?' he said, trying to search my face to find out the truth.

'You're okay, you think?'

'I think I need a drink,' he said.

'Why don't you help yourself,' I suggested, and he nodded gratefully. He bypassed the lager and wine and went straight to the brandy.

'Are you sure you're okay?' I whispered as I watched him down the first one before pouring a second.

He shook his head, just as Matt began introducing the crowd to each other.

Charlie appeared from the loo and poured herself a glass of orange juice.

'Orange juice?' I laughed. 'That's not like you.'

Then it dawned on me, and I looked from her to Adam and back again.

'You're pregnant?' I whispered.

Charlie squealed and nodded. 'We were going to keep it a secret but now that you've guessed… Well, you all may as well know. We're going to have a baby.' She squealed again.

Adam just stood, clearly mortified, as everyone began passing on their congratulations to the excited blonde.

Matt stood, dumb-founded for a moment before he turned to Adam. 'Congratulations, mate. Well done,' he said, looking totally shocked. 'I wasn't expecting that,' he muttered.

'Yes, yes, congratulations,' I said, trying to hide the hurt I was feeling inside. A baby? They were going to have a baby? The one thing I could never have myself and she was pregnant. Carrying the baby I wished so badly could have been mine. Mine and Adam's. Yes, mine and Adam's, that was my first thought. Not mine and Matt's. Oh, God.

I turned away from everyone and walked out of the kitchen, up the stairs and into the bedroom, where I sat on the bed and sobbed.

Minutes later, Matt appeared beside me. 'I'm sorry, babe. I know how hard it is every time one of your friends gets pregnant,' he said, putting his arm around my shoulders. 'I thought you'd come to terms with it long ago?' he asked.

He had no idea why I was really crying, so I just nodded, 'I thought so, too. It's hard, knowing I'll never have a baby growing inside me, you know.'

'I know, darling, I know. Shhhhh,' he said, standing up and pulling me up with him.

'Now, come on, pull yourself together. We're having a party.

You need to get back into the party mood. Come on, let's go and have a drink. It'll make you feel better.'

I tried to smile and followed him before I stopped and turned towards the bathroom. 'I'd better just go and freshen up first. I'll be right down.'

He nodded and left me to it.

In the bathroom, I leaned forward to look at myself in the mirror. My eyes were a little bloodshot, and my eyeliner had slid down my cheeks a little, but other than that, nobody would notice. I wiped my cheeks and smiled. It was so fake. I just hoped everyone would be getting too drunk to notice. I forced my shoulders back and shook my head, trying to get the image of Adam and Charlie together out of my imagination. They were married, they could have a baby if they want one. Right?

As I walked downstairs, Adam was cradling another brandy and trying to get my attention. He nodded towards the back door. I shook my head. I didn't want to talk to him. I couldn't. He pleaded with his eyes and I eventually relented. Making sure everyone else was busy partying, I headed outside a few minutes after he disappeared.

He stood beside the bins at the side of the house, out of sight, in the darkness. I gingerly stepped towards him.

'A baby?' I whispered.

He took another gulp of his drink and looked like he wanted to smash the glass against the wall.

'I had no idea,' he said gruffly. 'We haven't,' he looked down. 'We haven't been close since... since.'

'It doesn't matter, Adam. She's your wife. I'm happy for you both.'

He looked up, surprised. 'Really? How could you be?'

'Oh Adam,' I said, leaning against the wall beside him and taking a long swig of my wine. 'Of course I'm not really happy about it. I'm devastated.'

'Oh babe,' he said, trying to pull me towards him.

'No,' I cried. 'Don't. Never again, remember?' I searched his eyes as we both thought back to the swimming pool. 'Especially not now. She's carrying your child. She's your wife, Adam. Not me.'

'I was... I was going to leave her,' he whispered.

A breath caught in my chest, and I struggled with my feelings for him.

'Wh...when?'

'I've been trying to do it since... since the manor. Jack...'

'Oh,' was all I could say.

'Jack made me see sense, Eve, and I knew that I couldn't continue this charade with Charlie. It isn't fair on her to stay when I'm...' he faltered. 'When I'm so deeply in love with another woman,' he said, looking away from me.

I gasped and put my hand to my chest. 'Oh, Adam. I...I feel the same way, but things are different, now.'

'I know.' He laughed mirthlessly. 'Now, I have to do the right thing for my child.'

'Yes,' I said, standing upright. 'You married her, you must love her, right? You can make it work.' I was saying everything I didn't want to say, but I knew it was the right thing to do. His child was more important than anything. His child was so precious.

He slowly nodded. 'I thought I loved her, Eve, but now I know it's not real love. There's only one real love in my life,' he whispered, stepping away from me. 'I'm sorry. I'm truly sorry,' he said, turning to look at me before he pushed open the kitchen door and walked inside without looking back again.

Real love? I knew exactly what he meant.

$\mathcal{M}$att was moping around the house again. He was beginning to drive me insane. 'Go for a ride,' I suggested. 'It's a nice enough day.'

He shrugged his shoulders.

'You haven't been since Charlie's doctor told her not to. It's her he said shouldn't do it, not you. What happened to all your other cycle buddies, anyway?' I asked irritated.

He shrugged.

'How about a motorbike ride? You haven't been out for a few weeks. Why not do that? I just want you to do something, Matt.'

He perked up a little bit.

'You could invite Howard to go with you?'

'Yes, I suppose,' he muttered.

'What's the matter with you, babe? Something's eating you.'

'Nothing, I'm fine, really. Must be the weather or something.'

I glanced outside – at the unusually bright blue sky for March – and arched my eyebrows. 'It's a beautiful day out there, why would it be the weather?'

'Maybe the moon, then,' he said, half smirking at me.

I laughed. 'Oh yes, you're one of those people affected by the moon. Must be that. Do you want me to go out with you?'

He raised his eyebrows. 'You want to go out on the bike?'

I shrugged. 'If it makes you feel better.'

Matt smiled. 'It's a nice idea, but making you miserable won't really help matters, will it? Maybe I'll just go out for a ride for a bit.'

'That's the spirit.' I smiled. At last, a decision. Maybe I could try and get some work done in the meantime.

He disappeared into the garage and after five minutes, re-emerged with his helmet in his hands. He looked as if he was in slightly better spirits. I sat drinking a cup of tea at the kitchen table as he carefully cleaned his visor.

Then he went to put on his leathers, returning a few minutes later, all geared-up and ready to go. He was grinning.

'It's nice to see you smiling for a change,' I said as he bent over and pecked me on the lips.

'I'll see you in a few hours, then.'

'I'll be here. Just be careful.'

'I will,' he grinned.

'Love you,' I called out as the garage door slammed behind him. Minutes later, the deep burbling sound of his Yamaha R1 echoed throughout the house. I went to the front door and watched him close the garage door before he climbed back on and rode down the road at a higher speed than he should have been driving – at least down our street, anyway.

As I turned to go back inside, I spotted Charlie standing in her living room watching him drive away. She wiped the side of her face and then when she saw me, she looked a little embarrassed before waving and scurrying away.

Finally having the house to myself, I plodded up the stairs and walked into my office. It was my haven. Matt had decorated it for me within the last month. He'd done it exactly to my specification. I'd told him I wanted it to look like a forest, so he'd really gone to town. The most beautiful deep green forest wallpaper covered all four walls and a tall bookcase filled one side of the room. A thick dark green carpet covered the floor, and he'd taken special care installing a false ceiling, painted a deep shade of blue, which was filled with tiny holes. Lights above it made each hole twinkle like the most beautiful night sky. My desk was in one corner, so my back was against the wall when I worked. And from there I could see both the gorgeous forest and out of the window. Heavy blackout blinds wholly shut out any daylight if I wanted to just be in the dark; I tended to work better in the dark. I smiled every time I entered. Just being in there made me want to create a new book. Sadly though, my inspiration had come to an abrupt halt several months earlier. I wonder what caused it, I thought sarcastically as I closed the blinds and then lay on the floor, spreading my arms and legs out like a child as I looked up at my false sky.

I smiled, though, as I identified the constellations that Matt had created. Sometimes he could be particularly sweet, even lately, in between his dark moods. Moods that he didn't want to talk about. He was shutting me out. But then, isn't that what I had been doing before? We hadn't really talked for months.

I rolled over on to my side and looked at the old fashioned brown lamp I'd found in a second-hand shop in town. Most people thought it was ugly, but I saw the beauty in it immediately. It was moulded to look like leaves, and the second I'd spotted it, I knew it would be perfect for my office. Matt had looked at me as if I were mad when I'd brought it home, but when it was placed in the corner, it looked like it had been designed solely for that purpose. Even Matt had agreed it looked good.

I rolled forward onto my stomach and closed my eyes for a second. Maybe I could sleep for a little while, I thought, just as the doorbell rang. Groaning, I rolled over and stood up before switching off the lights and heading downstairs.

It was Charlie.

'Hey, Charlie,' I said, kissing her on the cheek. 'How are you?'

She leaned back with her hand on her lower back, accentuating the baby bump, which was flourishing. 'I'm not too bad, thanks, darlin'. A bit fed up of all this morning sickness, though.'

'I can imagine,' I said as I moved out of the way so she could come in. 'It's good to see you. We haven't seen much of you, lately. Would you like a cup of tea? I've actually got some ginger tea if you fancy it?'

'Ooh, darlin', that'd be lovely, thanks. The doctor recommended I have ginger whenever I feel a bit nauseous.'

'Come on through,' I said as she followed me into the kitchen and yawned loudly.

'Ooh, sorry. I've just been so tired lately. I had no idea pregnancy played such havoc.' She smiled sadly. 'Oh, Eve, I'm sorry,' she said. 'You must think I'm so insensitive, talking about being pregnant.'

'Don't be silly, Charlie. I'm delighted for you, and you can talk about being pregnant as much as you like. I came to terms with it a long time ago.'

'Really?' she asked. 'It's just that you seemed so upset when I told you I was expecting.'

I stopped for a second, hovering the ginger tea bag over the cup before dropping it in. 'Well, occasionally, it is hard. But it was more of a shock than anything. What with Adam having adult children, I guess I just wasn't expecting it, that's all.'

Charlie remained quiet for a while.

'Here you go. Careful, it's hot,' I said as I handed her the cup. 'Would you like a biscuit?'

'No, thanks.'

'You sure? I've got Ginger Nuts?' I winked.

'Oh, if you insist then,' Charlie grinned and I pulled the unopened packet out of the cupboard.

'I'm surprised they haven't been opened yet, they're Matt's favourite. They don't usually last this long.'

'Oh, really?' Charlie asked.

'He's not himself at the moment. I don't know what's wrong,' I sighed, taking a sip of my own Rooibos tea.

'Isn't he? Maybe it's the weather?' she suggested.

'Funny, he said the same thing. But the weather's perfect. For March, anyway.'

'Yes, I suppose so,' she said sadly.

'Are you okay, Charlie? You don't seem your usual perky self?' I smiled.

She looked out of the window for a moment before she shook her head. 'Oh, it's nothing. Probably just the pregnancy. Your hormones go crazy. It's not very nice,' she said quietly.

'Well, just a few more months to go, eh?'

'Just over two,' she muttered.

'Well not long then, not really.'

'I'm terrified,' she whispered.

'Oh Charlie, don't be,' I reassured her and sat down opposite.

'Adam said he'll be there but...but...'

'But what?' I asked.

'I don't really want him to be there.'

'Why ever not?'

Charlie shrugged her shoulders and looked a little embarrassed before speaking, 'I've already spoken to my sister, and she's promised to be there. I don't know, Eve. I just don't want him there.'

'Have you told him?' I asked.

'No... not yet.'

'I'm sure he'll understand.'

'Maybe.' She mused for a moment, and then, all of a sudden, asked, 'Where's Matt gone?'

'Just out for a ride. He was getting on my nerves, so I suggested it. He hasn't been out for a while. It'll do him good.'

'Yes, it will.' She smiled.

'I think he misses you,' I said, laughing.

Charlie's face turned pink, and she almost dropped her tea.

'Oh, careful. It's hot,' I said, going to grab it.

'Sorry. What do you mean, he misses me?' She whispered as I wiped the little bit of spilt liquid from the table.

'Cycling,' I said. 'He likes going riding with you.'

'Yes, me too,' she replied shyly. 'I miss it too.'

Suddenly standing up and heading into the hall, she said, 'I'd better go. Thanks for the tea, Eve. Maybe see you soon?'

Before I had a chance to answer her, she was out the door, closing it behind her.

Weird.

CHAPTER 12

I'd whipped up a chicken madras – Matt's favourite – for dinner, but by half-past seven I was starting to get worried. He rarely stayed out on the motorbike this long. I paced up and down the hallway, trying to get him on the mobile – knowing full well that he wouldn't answer it if he was driving. Cursing him under my breath, I decided I'd just go ahead and eat before him. Sod him. If he was this late, then he'd just have to re-heat it when he eventually got home.

I was just plating up when the doorbell went. Did he forget his keys? He never forgot his keys.

I put the saucepan of rice back on the side and headed to the front door. My heart did a flip as I opened it. A policeman stood staring back at me.

'Mrs. Brooke?' he asked, holding his hat in his hands and turning it around and around. 'I'm afraid there's been an accident,' was all I heard before I fell to the floor.

oOo

'Eve? Eve?' said a worried voice I recognised.

'Charlie? Wh...what happened?" I asked before I spotted the same police officer standing behind her in the hallway.

85

'You collapsed,' she said with tears in her eyes.

'What's happening? Where's Matt?' I asked. 'What happened to Matt?'

'I'm afraid he was involved in a crash, Mrs Brooke.'

'Is he... is he...' Charlie whispered, holding on to the stairs.

'He's alive,' was all the police officer said, as Charlie and I both burst into tears.

'He's at the Royal United Hospital...'

'Eve! Eve!' shouted a voice from the driveway before Adam rushed in past the policeman, his face a mask of fear.

'Charlie? What's happened? Eve? Are you alright?' he said as he rushed to my side and kneeled beside me.

'It's Matt,' Charlie whispered, trying to hold back more tears from falling. 'He's been in an accident.'

'How bad is it? Where is he?' he asked, standing and turning to look at the police officer.

'He's at A&E at the Royal United Hospital, sir. I'm afraid I can't tell you anything else. That's all I know.'

'Thank you, officer. We'll go right away. Thank you.'

'Are you alright?' he asked, and I nodded.

'Yes, thank you,' I said, in shock as he nodded and turned to leave, closing the door behind him.

'Come on, put some shoes on. I'll drive,' Adam said as he helped me to my feet.

'I'm coming too,' Charlie cried, stumbling behind us.

oOo

'I'M SORRY, but only Mrs Brooke is permitted to enter the room at the moment,' said a young male nurse.

Adam nodded as Charlie wailed beside him, sobbing into her handkerchief.

'Charlie, for goodness' sake,' he said to her. 'Pull yourself together, and go and sit down, would you?'

She wiped her tear-stained face and looked away from him in disgust.

He sighed as he took her arm and helped her to the nearest seat, where she struggled to get comfortable; big wet tears continued to stream down her face.

I followed the nurse into the room where Matt was being treated. Unprepared for what I was about to see, I almost collapsed at the sight of him.

He hadn't yet been cleaned of the blood, and his head was being supported by a neck brace.

'Matt? Matt?' I cried, 'Can you hear me?'

'Eve,' said a little voice from beyond the brace.

'Oh, thank God,' I whispered as I approached his head.

'I don't know what's happening, I can't see,' his voice was broken, and tears slid down the sides of his face.

I'd never seen him cry before, apart from a couple of really sad movies, but that didn't really count. My heart broke in that very instant.

'Oh, Matt. How are you feeling? Are you in pain?' I asked, as one of the nurses cleaning the blood from his limbs smiled at me.

'He shouldn't be, now that he has some morphine in his system,' she offered.

'What's wrong with him? Do you know what happened?' I asked.

'Apparently, he T-boned a car. I think he was going quite fast. He's lucky to be alive. There are a couple of obvious broken bones, but we're just waiting to take him for a scan to determine the extent of his injuries. Don't worry, my love, we'll take care of him.'

I smiled gratefully. 'Thank you. Matt, did you hear that? You're being well looked after,' I said, trying to be strong.

'Don't nod, keep your head straight. Until we can rule out a neck or spinal injury, you must stay straight. Do you understand, Matt?' asked another nurse who had appeared with an orderly behind him. 'We're taking him for the scan right now, love,' he said to me. 'Why don't you go back to the waiting room and we'll come and get you when he's back?'

I nodded.

'Don't worry, he's in excellent hands.' He smiled.

'I'll be right here when you get back, okay, Matt? I'm right here. I'm not going anywhere.'

'Charlie?' he asked suddenly.

'No, it's me, Eve,' I said. 'Charlie's here though, with Adam. He drove me here, Charlie came with us.'

'Charlie,' he whispered again, as he was rolled out of the room.

'Yes, Charlie,' I said.

I didn't think anything about it. He'd just had a really nasty accident, he was bound to be confused. I followed him out and then walked back into the waiting room, where Adam was sitting beside his wife, who was still crying. Hormones really do make you emotional, I figured.

She tried to stand up when she spotted me.

'Well?' she almost demanded. 'Is he okay? Is he going to be okay? Tell me, Eve. Tell me.'

I sat down and nodded. 'He's in good hands. He's got a couple of broken bones, but they won't know the extent of his injuries until he's had the scan. They just took him for it now. I don't know how long it'll take, but they're going to come and get me when he's finished,' I said, as I began to cry again.

Adam stood up and pulled me towards him. 'He'll be alright, Eve,' he said, tenderly rubbing my back. 'Don't worry.'

'It was my idea he go for a ride,' I sobbed into his shoulder. 'He wouldn't be in this state now if it wasn't for me.'

'You can't blame yourself, silly. Shhhh,' he reassured.

His touch was like a hot bath, and my muscles began to relax beneath his fingers. I sighed and then suddenly stepped away from him, looking around for Charlie, but she wasn't there.

Adam gently took hold of my arm and led me to a chair. 'Sit down. I'll go and get us a sweet tea. Charlie? Do you want some tea...? Oh, she must've gone to the loo,' he said as he wandered off in search of a cafeteria.

It seemed like ages after we'd drunk a cup of tea that Charlie finally appeared, with dark rings under her eyes.

'Charlie, where on Earth have you been? You're seven months pregnant, you can't just disappear like that. We were worried,' he said, standing up and helping her to a seat.

'I just went for a walk,' she whispered. 'I couldn't just stay here and do nothing. I found where they do the scans...'

'Charlie, why would you do that?' he asked.

'I want answers, Adam. I want to know if he's going to be okay.'

'And?'

'They wouldn't tell me anything, because I'm not a...not a...relative. I'm not his...his... w-wife.'

'Exactly why you should have just stayed here and relaxed. It can't be good for the baby to be pacing up and down hospital corridors,' he scolded.

I zoned out and closed my eyes, hoping I might drop off to sleep, but it was useless, there was too much noise. People coming and going, machines beeping, phones ringing, and so on. And that smell... it was horrible. The stench of sickness and extreme cleanliness combined. It wasn't doing my stomach any good. Maybe it was good that I hadn't had any dinner; otherwise, I might just have thrown up all over the floor.

I pinched the bridge of my nose; my head was starting to hurt, and my shoulders were so tense that the ache was threatening to run down my entire back. God, listen to yourself. Your husband is lying there half dead, and you're moaning about a little headache. Pull yourself together, woman.

I opened my eyes and looked around, just as the nurse appeared with a smile. 'Mrs. Brooke?' he asked, and I nodded.

Charlie stood up, 'Can I see him?' she begged.

Adam shook his head and looked away, embarrassed.

'I'm sorry, only Mrs Brooke can see him at the moment. 'He turned back to me. 'Follow me.'

I followed him through into a different room, and this time Matt had been cleaned up. His bike gear was gone, and he was wearing one of those awful hospital gowns. A brace of a different kind was wrapped around his neck, and another nurse was busy treating some of his other injuries.

'He's going to be just fine,' she said. 'The scan showed nothing we should worry about.'

'But why the neck brace?' I asked as I sat down in the chair they'd kindly placed beside him. I carefully took his non-bandaged hand in mine.

'Whiplash,' she said. 'A broken wrist, a small break in his ankle, and plenty of bruises. I'm afraid you'll be unable to, erm, partake in any sexual activity for a few weeks though.' She smiled apologetically.

'What?' said Matt, suddenly perking up a little.

'You have quite a lot of swelling in the nether regions. It's very common in motorbike accidents, unfortunately.'

'Bruised bollocks?' he asked, and I cringed.

'Very bruised,' she grinned at me. 'Don't worry, though, most men heal quite quickly and can usually resume full sexual function in no time. You'll be fine. You need to be careful with your neck, wrist and ankle for a while, though.'

'Can I go home?' he asked.

'That's up to the doctor to say, but you'll probably be here for a couple of days. Don't worry, it's just a precautionary measure.'

I nodded. 'Thank you,' I said as she finished up and walked out, leaving me alone with him.

'Oh, Matt. What happened?' I asked, peering at his eyes, which were quite bloodshot.

'A car pulled out on me.'

'So it was his fault?'

'Of course,' he said.

'But you were speeding?' I assumed.

When he said nothing, I knew the answer, but there was no point arguing about that now. What was done was done.

CHAPTER 13

I drove myself to the hospital the next day, taking Matt's favourite chocolates and a couple of cycling magazines with me. I almost bought a motorbike magazine as well, but then thought better of it.

As I entered the room where he had been moved to, I was surprised to see a woman I didn't recognise. In her arms was a baby.

'Oh, sorry,' I said, 'I must've got the wrong room.' But as I went to turn away, I noticed that it was Matt sitting upright in the bed. 'Oh.'

'Hey, Eve,' he said. 'This is Kristen, Charlie's sister.'

'Oh, hi, Kristen. It's nice to meet you.'

'Eve,' said a voice behind me.

I turned to see Charlie, smiling at me.

'My sister came to take me baby clothes shopping, so we thought we'd pop in to see the patient. I'm so happy to see him doing okay.' She grinned.

'I know, it's such a relief, isn't it?' I said, turning to Matt and smiling, pecking him briefly on the lips. 'How are you feeling?'

'Like I've been run over by a bus,' he said. I was just about to put the magazines on his bed when I noticed the very same ones were already there.

'Oh,' I said, a little disappointed. I just handed him the chocolates instead. 'I was going to get you a biker magazine but thought better of it.' I smiled.

'I doubt I'll be biking for a while. Besides, the R1's been written off.'

'Oh, I'm sorry, babe.'

'I'll buy a new one when the insurance comes through.'

I shook my head and turned back to Kristen and Charlie. 'And who is this little one?'

Kristen smiled. 'Johnny.'

'He's gorgeous,' I said.

'Thank you. Well, Charlie,' she said through gritted teeth, elbowing her sister, 'we should go.

'Yes, we should,' Charlie replied but didn't move from Matt's side.

'Sis,' Kristen insisted.

'Oh, yeah, right, yes. Let's make a move. Matt, it's so good to see you, babe. Take care. Hope to see you home soon enough,' she said, lingering over him a little.

Matt looked at her and smiled. 'Hopefully, we can get back in the saddle soon?'

I laughed, looking at the heavily pregnant woman and the man in several casts and a neck brace. 'Something tells me that isn't going to happen anytime soon.'

Charlie laughed a little too hard. 'No, no, probably not,' she said before she kissed him gently on one cheek and then swiftly on the other one.

Turning to me, she kissed both my cheeks and walked out.

'Nice to meet you, Eve. Matt,' said Kristen, who quickly followed her sister out into the corridor.

I breathed a long sigh and went to sit beside my husband, who shifted his weight in the bed.

'Are you uncomfortable? Can I help to re-arrange your pillows or something?'

'No, no, Charlie fluffed them up for me. I'm fine. Just fed up of lying down. that's all.'

'Hopefully, you'll be able to come home soon. Have you spoken to the doctor?'

'Yes, Dr Johnson was here just before you arrived. He said I can leave tomorrow, so will you come and pick me up first thing? I can't wait to get out of here.'

'Of course.'

'Will you bring my car? I don't think I'll be very comfortable in yours.'

I nodded. 'No problem. Is there anything you need in the meantime?'

He tried to shake his head and winced. 'I keep forgetting I can't move my head. No, I'm fine. Have you spoken to the guys at work?'

'I actually forgot until Howard rang earlier this morning.'

Matt tensed for a second. 'What did he say?'

'Nothing. I just told him what happened. He said he'd stop by around half-past ten. Oh, it's almost ten-thirty now. He'll probably be here any second. And talk of the devil,' I said, as Howard appeared in the doorway carrying a balloon and a little blue teddy bear that said Get Well Soon on it.

We both laughed at the sight of him. 'Thanks, Howard,' Matt chuckled.

'Alright, Eve?' he asked, as I stood up to accept his hug.

'I'm fine, thanks. Just a little fed up of Matt having all these accidents. First the bicycle and then this,' I smiled, sitting back down.

'Bicycle?' Howard asked, looking a little confused.

'Yes,' Matt interrupted quickly. 'Remember when I crashed the bike in the storm and stayed overnight at yours?'

Howard looked a little taken aback before he looked at me and then back at Matt.

'Storm, oh yes, of course.' He laughed strangely. 'I'd clearly gone and forgotten all about that. Yes, yes, the accident. The storm.'

I watched them both and shook my head. Blokes were so weird sometimes.

'Right, I'll leave you to it. You two have probably got work to discuss, anyway. Hopefully, Matt won't need too much time off.' I chuckled. 'Shall I come back later, darling?'

'No, no need, Eve. Just come and pick me up in the morning. I'll probably just sleep the rest of the day, anyway. Won't be particularly good company.'

'Alright, if you're sure?'

'I'm sure,' he said, as I squeezed his good hand and kissed him on the forehead. I picked up my handbag and headed out the door.

'So how are you feeling, blue balls?' Howard joked as I walked out and shook my head, chuckling.

CHAPTER 14

Matt's new nickname was Buster Gonad. I couldn't help it. When I first saw him naked after the accident, his balls were massive due to the swelling. Not only that, but they were black and blue. It was a little worrying, but just before we left the hospital a few days before, Dr Johnson had assured us both that it was nothing to worry about.

Naturally, though, Matt was worried sick. 'What if I can't get it up any more?' he kept asking. 'Then what will I do? Life won't be worth living if I can't get it up,' he cried.

I was really mean and just laughed. If the doctor said it was nothing to worry about, then there was nothing to worry about. But two days had passed, and both mornings he had awoken without his normal erection.

'Ring the doctor if you're so worried about it,' I said when I got fed up hearing him moaning about it.

'I will, I'll just give it one more day.'

The next morning, Matt shook me awake at six o'clock with a big grin on his face.

'Check this out. Come on boyo,' he said, pulling back the covers to reveal an erection to rival all erections.

'Great,' I said, rolling back over and falling back to sleep again.

When the alarm went off an hour later, I turned around to see him struggling to get dressed, ready to go back to work.

'You're going to work? Isn't it a bit too soon?' I asked.

He shook his head, 'Howard's picking me up. I can work alright, I just can't drive with this bloody thing on,' he said, pointing to the neck brace.

'And that,' I said, pointing to his ankle. 'And that,' I pointed to his wrist.

'Yeah, I suppose. But as long as Howard drives, I can boss people about.' He grinned. 'Can you give me a hand with my shirt?'

I climbed out of bed and helped button up the warm lumberjack shirt.

'You sure you'll be okay?' I asked, concerned.

'I'll be fine, don't worry,' he said, smiling.

'You certainly seem perkier this morning. It's amazing what a hard-on can do to a man.'

He grinned and went to leave the room. 'I'll see you later then. Have a good day.'

'Yeah, you too. See you later.'

I walked into the bathroom and sat on the loo. We seemed to have stopped kissing each other in the morning, and at night. And in between.

We were living this strange life where, apart from occasional seemingly meaningless sex (missionary position only), we were more like roommates. Friends with rather dull benefits, perhaps?

I listened to him open the front door, the sound of Howard's voice drifted up from downstairs, and then I heard them drive away down the street.

I flushed the loo and then climbed into the shower, where I stood letting the hot water penetrate deep into my muscles. It had been a while, but I suddenly felt the need to be touched. Needless to say, Adam popped into my mind. Even after everything that had happened, he was the only one that made me feel horny. Just the thought of him when I was naked was enough to make me desperate for an orgasm. I covered myself in shower gel and gently rubbed my arms and legs, my back then my chest. My hands hovered over my breasts as I thought about the night in the pool, how close we'd been to actually doing it. I remembered how his hands had touched me all over before his tongue came so close to licking me right where I desperately needed it to.

I slid my hands down over my belly, through the soft pubic hair until my fingers rested there. I groaned. I cupped myself for a moment before plunging my finger inside myself. My buttocks pushed forward against my hands, and I leaned forward onto the wall with one hand. It wasn't enough, though. I needed more.

So I rinsed myself off and towel dried before walking into the bedroom, opening the wardrobe searching around for my special box. I pulled out my favourite vibrator. It had cost a small fortune, but boy did it work. Matt and I used to use it together all the time.

I climbed on the bed and covered myself with the duvet, shutting out the light, then I switched it on to pulse and allowed my thoughts to drift to London, the one and only time Adam and I had ever had full-on sex. I say one and only time, but we'd actually done it almost all night long, so quite a few times in total. We'd done it in the shower and in the bath, on the desk in the hotel room, the floor, in front of the mirror and, eventually, in the bed.

The sensation intensified as I thought back to the evening we'd danced in the rain before heading to his house in the country. I let out a deep guttural groan as the vibrations sent my body into convulsions. I came more than once and then removed the device from my body and turned it off. Then I just lay there feeling guilty.

I should have been doing that with my husband, not with a bloody machine. I flipped back the covers and looked out of the window. It was such a grey day. Tears filled my eyes, as I thought about what was probably happening in the house next door.

Were they having early morning sex? I'd heard that pregnancy can increase all kinds of sensations during intercourse. I groaned and rolled over, trying to shake the image from my mind, but it wouldn't budge. All I could think about was Adam shoving himself deep inside her, doggie style. She'd have his fingers in her mouth while she touched herself with her own.

The thought made me feel warm down below. I hated it. Hated that such a horrible idea was still turning me on.

I screamed silently and threw the vibrator across the room. It hit the wardrobe and fell to the carpet with a thud.

I jumped off the bed and ran back towards it. Picking it up, I turned it back on and tiptoed to the window, where I knelt down so anyone looking could only see the top half of me. I couldn't care less if anyone saw me as I rubbed it against myself, my lower half gyrating against it. I didn't put it inside me this time, I just thought about Adam and rubbed it against my clitoris. As if reading my mind, their front door opened just as I started to come. He looked up at me, and I just stared as I came right in front of him. My mouth opened, and I groaned.

He looked shocked, gazing around and then back up at me. His face showed nothing but intense longing. I knew if he could, he would have climbed our stairs two at a time and fucked me long and hard, for the rest of the day. I stood up so he could see my naked self and stepped away from the window.

A couple of minutes later, I heard his tyres screeching as he drove away.

CHAPTER 15

The swelling had gone down, and the bruising was almost gone, but Matt had made no effort to have sex with me. Now we really were like roommates. Not even friends with benefits, anymore. We hadn't kissed each other for ages. He totally zoned out around me, but I'd got to the stage where I no longer cared. It suited me just fine. I was having an entirely pleasurable relationship with my vibrator, thank you very much.

Walking into the post office to send my mum's birthday present, I spotted Howard at the front of the queue. Smiling, I waited for him to finish and then stopped him as he went to walk out.

'Howard,' I said.

'Eve,' he replied, looking a little uneasy.

'Is everything alright?' I asked.

'Erm, Eve. I've been meaning to tell you something. I shouldn't have lied before. I hate keeping other people's sordid secrets, and Matt is in the wrong.'

'What are you talking about?' I whispered.

He pulled me out of the queue, and I followed him outside.

'I'm sorry, love, but I can't do it. That time Matt told you he'd had the accident in the storm?'

I nodded. 'It wasn't true?' I asked flabbergasted. Why on Earth would he lie to me?

Howard nodded. 'It was. He did have an accident, but he didn't stay with me that night, Eve. I'm so sorry to have to tell you. But I won't lie, not even for Matt. It's wrong. I'm sorry,' he said, dropping his eyes towards the ground.

'B...b-but where did he stay, Howard? If he wasn't with you, who was he with?'

Howard looked terribly guilty. 'I'm sorry, love, but he never told me. He wouldn't.'

'Oh, okay,' I said. 'Well, I appreciate you telling me the truth. Thank you, Howard,' I said, turning away and walking back into the post office, where I got back in the queue as if nothing had happened.

Just as I got to the front and handed the parcel over, my mobile rang. I ignored it. Whoever it was would ring back if it was important. I handled my business, sending the parcel to Portugal before I walked out in a bit of a daze.

I walked for a while, gazing into shop windows but not really seeing anything until I stopped in front of a baby shop. The cute outfits called out to me, and I smiled.

Pushing the door open, I wandered in and started pulling out all the newborn items. I finally settled on the cutest little yellow onesie, with matching socks and hat. I bought a small green teddy as well and then headed out to find where I'd parked the car. Where was it?

While I walked through the car park, my phone rang. I fumbled about in my handbag until I picked it up just as it rang off. There were eleven missed calls, all from Adam.

Sensing something was wrong, I called him as I climbed into my little car, carefully placing the beautifully wrapped parcel on the passenger seat.

'Adam?' I said when he picked up. He sounded breathless. 'What's wrong?'

'It's Charlie,' he muttered.

'What's happened?'

'Her waters broke, but she refused to let me take her to the hospital. She insisted I call Matt to take her.'

'Matt? Why would she want Matt?'

'Eve, I'm not sure. Look, I know she doesn't want me to be there during the birth, maybe because she doesn't want me to see her like that. I don't know. Just... I just feel like you should come with me.'

'You do?' I asked, overcome with confusion.

'Please. Where are you now?'

'I'm just leaving town.'

'I'll meet you in the car park at the hospital.'

'Okay, Adam, I'll be there as quickly as I can.' I put the phone down and immediately reversed out, heading for the hospital.

'Thanks for coming,' he said as I pulled up alongside him.

'No problem. But I don't understand what's going on. She probably needs as much support as possible, right now. I'm happy to be here for her... and you,' I added as I grabbed the little parcel before locking the car doors.

'I just bought this actually,' I said, handing it to him.

He smiled warmly. 'Thank you.'

Together we walked in, asking for directions to the labour ward. When we got there, Adam asked at the reception for Charlotte Grove.

'Oh, she's actually giving birth right now. But... erm,' the nurse looked embarrassed. 'The father is already in with her.'

'No, I'm afraid not.' Adam smiled nervously. 'I'm the father. I'm Charlie's... Charlotte's husband.'

'Oh, erm... Please just give me a moment,' she said, disappearing to probably find someone in charge.

After a few minutes, a large older woman appeared. 'Hello, I understand you're looking for your wife. Can I have her name, please?' she said, looking down at her papers.

'Charlotte Grove.'

'Right, she's in room sixteen but,' she said, placing her hand on Adam's arm, 'please understand that there is another man in there with her.'

'Oh, that's alright. That's my husband. We're all friends,' I said, smiling.

'Of course,' said the nurse. Please, follow me.

We both walked behind the woman until she stood in front of a cosy looking room. She pushed it open a little and peered inside.

'Oh, it seems like it was a quick labour,' she said, pushing the door open so Adam and I could walk in. But as we did, the first thing we saw was Eve with tears pouring down her face. Her face was lit up, and she was smiling. Matt turned around slowly, holding the tiniest little baby. A baby that looked exactly like him, with his shade of dark red hair.

'Son of a bitch,' Adam growled as he turned away. He looked at me and shook his head before he walked quickly away.

'Matt?' I muttered. 'Matt? Charlie?'

Neither of them said a word.

I literally felt like I'd been punched in the stomach. I turned, looking for the bathroom. Rushing down the corridor towards it, I only just reached the toilet when everything I'd eaten earlier came up. I retched until there was nothing left. And then I calmly washed my face and walked out of the hospital.

CHAPTER 16

Everything started to make sense. I felt like such a fool. It had been right in front of me, the whole time. There I was, trying so hard not to be with the man I loved more than anyone else, while his wife was busy screwing my husband.

I laughed as I drove through the busy streets, not really taking any notice where I was going. Soon I found myself out of town and speeding down country lanes. Eventually, I recognised a road I'd only been down once in my life. I switched on the indicator and turned in, driving until I came upon a broad set of gates. I parked the car just as it began to rain, not that I cared.

I walked through the little pedestrian gate beside the larger one and headed up the driveway until I stood in front of the large manor house that used to belong to Adam's Nana Grove. He wasn't there, of course, but I just didn't want to go home. So I sat on the grass in front of the house. After a couple of minutes, I lay down, facing up to the grey clouds that were dumping water all over me. Tears blended with the droplets of rain, and I shouted at the top of my voice, 'Fuck you! Fuck all of you!'

After about half an hour, I got to my feet and danced in the rain like some kind of crazy woman.

The sound of a car coming up the driveway scared the life out of me, and I stopped abruptly, almost falling over from dizziness.

A beautiful woman, about my age, with dark curly hair, climbed out and walked towards me. 'I'm guessing you're Eve,' she said.

I nodded breathlessly.

'We figured you might come here. Come on,' she said, putting her arm around my shoulders and leading me towards the main entrance. She pulled out the same set of keys that Adam had used a few months earlier, and I just stood, soaked to the bone, like a corpse. Not saying a word. Not moving a muscle. 'Eve,' she said. 'Let me get you a towel.'

Disappearing for a minute, she returned with a huge white towel which she gently placed over my shoulders. 'Come on.'

I followed her through into the large country kitchen, where she opened a cupboard and poured two glasses of wine.

'Come and sit down,' she instructed, handing me the drink. 'I'm Lisa,' she smiled.

'Lisa,' I whispered. 'Adam's ex?'

She nodded with a smile, taking a long sip of her drink.

'Why are you being so nice to me?'

'Adam is very dear to me. I will always love him – not in that way though, don't worry.'

'I don't understand. How did you know who I was? I was acting like some kind of insane person. You should have called the police or something. I would've done.'

'Adam called me when he left the hospital. He was in a bit of a state, as you can imagine. He was worried about you.'

'He was?'

'Of course, Eve.'

'Then why didn't he come?'

'I told him not to,' she stated, pushing the wine in front of me. 'Drink. It'll help.'

I took a long swig. 'I don't suppose you've got something stronger?'

Lisa laughed and stood up. 'Sure. Brandy? Whisky?'

'Brandy, please,' I said gratefully.

'The good stuff is in the bar. Give me a sec. On second

thoughts, let's go and sit in there, I can put the fire on. You'll be able to get drier quicker. We wouldn't want you to get a cold, now.'

Nodding, I stood up and followed her, with the towel dragging along the floor behind me.

'I told him not to come because I was worried he'd end up crashing the car or something. He's already started on the brandy too.' She smiled reassuringly, looking behind her as we walked through the vast lounge. 'So I told him I'd come and find you.'

'But how did you know to come here?'

'Adam waited for you to come home, and when you didn't, he just had a feeling this is where you would come. He was right. He's often right about you. It's like a sixth sense or something.'

'It is?' I whispered, warming myself in front of the grand gas fire that looked more like a real log fire.

'All those holidays you went on, and he just happened to be there at the same time?'

'He told you about that?'

Lisa nodded. 'It's fate, trying to get the two of you together.'

'You think so?' I asked as I started to feel a little woozy.

She nodded. 'Don't you?'

'Just a series of bizarre coincidences, probably.'

'Oh, Eve. You're even called Eve, and he's called Adam. How many coincidences do you want?

'How about his wife having my husband's baby?'

Lisa chuckled bitterly. 'Well, yes, that's a cruel twist of fate, that is.'

'You can say that again. Especially on account of my ovaries and womb being cut out of me ten years ago.' I snorted.

'Oh, really? Honey, I'm so sorry. I didn't know about that. That's awful.'

'It's all so fucked up,' I added, looking into the fake fire, my eyes getting heavy.

'You can say that again.'

'What now?' I asked. 'What happens now?'

Lisa looked puzzled. 'Isn't it obvious?'

'Should it be?'

'You and Adam live happily ever after.'

I shook my head. 'I don't think so.'

'Why ever not, Eve?'

'Everything's too fucked up for us to be happy. How can we possibly be happy after all this shit? It's like one of those crazy movies, for God's sake.'

'You're right about that,' Lisa said, leaning back in her seat before asking, 'but you love him, don't you?'

'That's not important anymore.'

'Of course it is.'

I shook my head. 'Lisa, you really are sweet, but life isn't all buttercups and fairies. I can't live with myself like this, not at the moment.'

'Christ, Eve. Don't do anything crazy, woman.'

I laughed and turned to look up at her from where I was hugging my knees to my chest on the floor. 'Don't worry, I wasn't thinking about hanging myself or anything. I just think I need some time on my own, you know? Maybe I need a break away from everyone. To get my head together. Think about what I want for myself. Think about my future, you know?'

'Yes, I do. I understand perfectly, and I think that's actually quite a good idea. But for now, I think you and Adam need to talk. Actually, I think you and Adam need to do more than talk.' She winked.

'God, this is just so bizarre,' I said.

'What's that?'

'You suggesting I need to have a hot and steamy sex session with your ex-husband.'

Lisa threw her head backwards and laughed a long throaty laugh. 'Eve, I do like you, and personally, I think you and Adam are perfect for each other.'

A deep sigh escaped from my lips, and I smiled before it turned into a grimace, recalling the look on Matt's face as he turned around to reveal he'd become a father with another woman.

This time it was a sob that escaped my lips and tears began to fall again.

'It's okay, honey. Just let it all out. Let me pour you another drink. You can stay here tonight. I'll stay too if you like. Or I can leave you alone if you prefer?'

'Stay, please stay,' I sobbed.

She nodded and gently squeezed my shoulder.

CHAPTER 17

*L*isa held my hair back as I puked into the toilet bowl for the fourth time the following morning. I was no longer embarrassed. We'd stayed up drinking for much of the night, but finally called it a night at about three, or so she told me. I'd had way too much to drink; I felt dismal. I would have preferred to stay in bed and hide under the covers for the rest of the day, but Lisa insisted I face the world. She was right, of course. I had to do it. I had to start making changes to my life so that I could continue it on my own. Become my own independent woman.

I'd been too drunk to think about it all last night, and too hungover this morning, but I knew I had to go home. Sooner rather than later.

Lisa was an absolute angel. She really cared. I had other friends, of course, but none that I could talk to the way we had talked the night before. Overnight, she'd become my new best friend.

I hugged her at the door and thanked her profusely for everything.

'Will you be alright?' she asked, as she locked the front door.

'Probably not,' I said, holding my stomach.

'You gonna be sick again?' she asked.

I shook my head. 'No, I don't think so.'

'Well, you've got my number and email now, so if you need to talk, any time, just call me. And I wrote down my address and put it in your pocket, so you can pop by any time. Remember that, Eve. We're going to be good pals, from now on, and I don't want you to have to go through any more shit on your own, you got it?' she asked like only a mum would. Probably because she'd raised two terrific kids of her own.

I nodded. 'Lisa, thank you for everything. Well, I'd better go and face the music.'

'You'll be okay. Call me later, okay?'

I nodded as I walked back down the driveway to my car. Shivering, I climbed in. It was freezing, so I whacked up the heating and slowly reversed back down the rest of the driveway, turning around at the bottom, before I drove back onto the main road and headed home.

As I eventually turned into my own driveway, I noticed Adam's bedroom blinds were still closed. He'd probably be sleeping off his own hangover.

Matt's car was parked, badly, just off the kerb and I cursed under my breath. I didn't want to see him. I hated him so much at that moment, and I would have preferred to rid myself of the feeling before I confronted him. But that wasn't going to happen. I got out of the car and walked up to the front door. Pushing it open, I found Matt sitting on the floor by the bottom of the stairs. My hatred fell away the second I laid eyes on him.

His face was filled with so much remorse; he was racked with guilt. How could I be so angry with him when I had been fighting my own feelings about Adam?

'Eve,' he cried, standing up. 'I didn't know if you'd come back. I was worried sick. I called you so many times.'

I dropped my handbag onto the hallway floor. 'I know. I threw the phone in the back of the car. I couldn't talk to you, Matt.'

'Evie, babe,' he said, carefully lifting his hand to move a stray hair out of my eye. 'I'm sorry. I should have told you everything. I should have come clean. We both know things haven't been right between us for so long, but this... this was... unforgivable. I'm so sorry. Charlie hates herself right now, too.'

'Yeah, I know how that feels,' I said, pushing his hand away and walking into the kitchen. I went towards the kettle, but Matt carefully pushed me aside and made me sit down.

'Let me do it. Tea with a little milk, right? I should make it sweet, yeah?' he said kindly.

I nodded. 'Not too sweet. I've spent the past couple of hours hugging the toilet bowl.'

'Oh, babe.'

I held my hand up. 'Please don't call me babe anymore, Matt. It just seems wrong.'

'Yeah, okay. I get it.'

'So how long has it been going on?' I asked, not really wanting to know, but needing to nonetheless.

He stiffened and turned to face me. 'You don't want to know, Eve. You're better off not knowing all the details.'

I shook my head. 'I need to, Matt. I don't want to, I just need to know. Just tell me and get it over with.'

He slowly nodded. 'It was instant between us. The moment she came over that night when they came to introduce themselves. It was like I'd been hit by a bus or something. It was the same for her.'

I nodded; I knew what that was like.

'But we tried to fight it, ba... Eve. We did try, but it was just so strong...'

'Or you were too weak?'

'Yeah, probably a bit of that, too. I'm so sorry. I hope one day you'll forgive us both. We didn't mean for this to happen. And then, then she...'

'Got pregnant?'

He stiffened again and nodded.

'Why didn't you tell us then, Matt? It was cruel to let Adam think the baby was his. Cruel.'

'I know, but we didn't know. We didn't know if it was mine or Adam's.'

'Well, we certainly don't need a DNA test to prove paternity, do we? I saw the baby, Matt. It looks exactly like you.'

'Yes, she does,' he whispered.

'She? It's a girl?' I asked, as a lone tear began to bulge out of the inner corner of my eye and dropped suddenly down the side of my nose.

'Yes, a little girl.' He smiled.

'Does she have a name?' I asked.

'Charlie has an idea, but I'm not sure it's the right thing to do. We wanted to run it by you first.'

'Why me?'

'Charlie knows that you can't have children, so she wants to call her... Evelyn.'

'Oh Matt that's kind of twisted, don't you think? But kind of sweet too, I guess. God, this is so fucked up.'

'I know.'

'What are we going to do?' I asked, not really thinking.

Matt shrugged. 'What do you want to do?'

'Well, we'll have to start divorce proceedings, naturally,' I said matter-of-factly. 'And we'll have to sell the house.'

'Yes, yes,' he said.

'I'm so confused at the moment, Matt. I'd really like it if you could leave the house for a while. Actually, no. I'm going to leave,' I said, thinking about Adam right next door. I needed to get away from everyone.

'No, you don't need to. I'll pack my things and go. Give you some time.'

I held my hand up, 'No, I'll go and stay with Mum and Dad for a while. Perhaps, while I'm there, you can put the house on the market. It shouldn't take long to sell. I'll give the lawyer Power of Attorney so you can sell to the first person who shows any interest. I'll pack my things before I go,' I said, speaking more to myself than to Matt. I was hiding my emotion, thinking solely on a practical level. 'You'll have to have the cat. She can't come with me.'

'Absolutely. Anything, Eve. Anything. Just tell me what you want me to do, and I'll do it.'

I want you to rewind time and not have a baby with the fucking neighbour, screamed the devil on my shoulder, but I shrugged it off and just smiled sadly. 'Yes, yes.'

'I'll leave for a few days while you pack. Just call me and let me know when your flight is. I could take you to the airport if you like?'

I nodded, tears welling up in my eyes. 'No, I want to leave now. Right now. Let me throw a few things together, and you can drive me straight to the airport.'

Matt looked at me, his eyes wide with surprise, 'Are you sure?' he asked.

I nodded, I wasn't sure about anything, anymore. All I knew is that I wanted to leave. I wanted to get out of that house, away from them, away from their baby, away from my life as I knew it.

oOo

'HEY, LISA, IT'S ME.'

'Hey, babe. How are you feeling?'

'Not great. I just wanted to ring you and let you know what I'm doing. I've decided to go and see my parents for a while. I need to get away, you know?'

'I know, hon. I understand. When are you leaving?'

'I'm at the airport right now.'

Lisa chuckled, on the other end of the phone. 'You don't mess about, do you?'

'If I gave it too much thought, I'd probably just carry on as normal, and I don't want that.'

'Of course not, and you shouldn't just plod on, either. You deserve a life, Eve. Happiness.'

'Happiness? What is that? I've forgotten what it feels like.'

'Oh, babe. You'll feel it again. You just need some time, I guess.'

'Time on my own, yeah. I think it'll do me good.'

'Absolutely. Have you seen Matt yet?' she asked.

I nodded. 'Yeah, he was waiting for me at the house.'

'And?'

'He was distraught.'

'He was distraught? What about you, Eve?'

'I just don't know, Lisa. I don't know anything, anymore. You

113

should have seen the look in his eyes. He's devastated about what he's done to me. I could see that.'

'Well, he bloody well should be, that asshole,' she said, and I chuckled. 'Hey, are you sure you're going to be okay?'

'No, not really, but I'll figure this out. Look, I'd better go, my flight's boarding already.'

'Okay, honey. Ring me in a few days and let me know how you are, okay?'

'I will, and Lisa?'

'Yeah, hon?'

'Thanks for being such a great friend.'

'Always here you for you, babe. Try and get some rest. Speak soon.'

I hung up the phone and smiled before I headed towards my departure gate.

CHAPTER 18

Standing on the clifftop at Sagres, I took a lungful of oxygen and sighed it out slowly through my lips. Blue was all I could see. The sea was green-blue up close but deepened in colour the further out I looked, and the sky just went on forever, not a single cloud to be seen.

Turning, I watched as my parents huddled together out of the wind. I knew they were confused, but I'd insisted I wouldn't say another thing on the matter when they'd pressed me a week before at the airport...

'But, my love. What about Adam? He's the one you...'

I'd held up my hand and shook my head. 'Mum, not a word. Don't you get it? I don't want to talk about it. Not with you, not with anyone. Just let me have some peace while I figure out what I'm going to do, okay?'

She'd sighed and reluctantly nodded, rubbing my shoulders. 'Whatever you want. You can stay as long as you need to. I've set up the spare bedroom upstairs, alright? It's yours for as long as you need it.'

Unable to stop the tears, I had nodded, and she'd hugged me close. It was the first time she'd done that for years; it felt good. Dad, a little lost, had stepped forward and hugged us both. People stared as the three of us, stood there in the middle of Faro airport, holding each other as tears flowed down my cheeks.

'Now, stop those tears, sweetheart,' Mum said, as she pulled away and wiped my cheeks with her handkerchief. 'Come on, George. Grab her bag and let's go. Let's go home. Okay?' she asked, turning to me.

I didn't say a word, I just nodded. We didn't always see eye to eye, but I was so lucky that Joyce and George Baggin were my parents.

That had been a week ago, and after spending a few days in my pyjamas watching daytime television, Dad insisted we get out of the house for a few hours. Trying to include me in life, they insisted I chose where to go.

'Sagres. I want to go to Sagres.'

Heading back towards them and pulling my woolly jumper close to my body, I could barely breathe, the wind was so strong. But it was exhilarating, feeling it biting into my face. My long hair was getting more and more tangled as it whipped about my head, but I just let it. I couldn't care less about what I looked like.

Mum grimaced when I approached. 'Look at the state of you,' she tutted, smiling and rummaging around in her handbag. 'Here,' she handed me a hairbrush as I climbed into the back seat of their old Peugeot. 'You'd better brush your hair before we stop for a bite to eat.'

Dutifully, I tried to run the brush through my locks, but the knots were everywhere. I relaxed back and looked out the window, watching as the sea disappeared behind us.

'Wait!' I yelled, spotting something along the road.

'What?' Mum cried. 'What is it?'

'Dad, can you pull over?'

'Why ever do you want us to do that?' she asked as Dad stopped the car in a nearby parking space.

'There's a coffee shop over there. You and Dad go for a coffee. There's just something I need to do. I won't be long, I hope.'

'Wh..wh...' Mum muttered, but Dad shushed her and nodded. 'Yes, dear.' Mum smiled at me. 'We'll go for a coffee in there.'

I grabbed my handbag and ran back down the street, walking into the salon I'd spotted.

'Hi. Do you speak English?' I asked the stylist who was sitting inside reading a Portuguese magazine.

She nodded and smiled. 'A little.'

'Great,' I immediately sat down. 'Cut it, please.'

'A trim?' she said, in near-perfect English.

I shook my head. 'No. Cut it. All of it.'

She looked a little taken aback before grinning. 'Of course.'

oOo

'Evelyn? Evie? No, what have you done? Your beautiful hair!' Mum cried, standing up and rushing towards me, her hands covering her mouth as she shook her head. 'Your beautiful hair,' she cried again and again.

Feeling somewhat liberated, I grinned mischievously. 'Don't you like it?' I asked, knowing full well she hated it.

Dad approached us with a smile, 'Sweetheart, I think you look beautiful. It brings out your cheekbones,' he said, kissing me on the cheek. 'Shall we go?'

'Oh, Eve. Why? Why would you do something like that?' Mum kept saying in the car.

I just sat back, finding the hairbrush beneath my fingers.

'I won't be needing this anymore, Mum,' I laughed, handing it to her in the front.

'Oh, Evie,' she muttered under her breath.

'Where would you like to go for lunch?' Dad asked, trying to change the subject.

Mum just shrugged, so he looked at me through the rearview mirror. 'Honey?'

'Lagos somewhere? Or shall we just head back home?' I suggested.

'No, let's not go home just yet. Lagos it is,' he said, as he read-justed his sitting position, and we drove the next thirty minutes in silence.

Eventually pulling up into a large car park, we climbed out of the car and started walking towards the marina, where a multitude of restaurants and cafes were located. Rounding the corner, I smiled at the sight of all the boats. It'd been a while since I visited Lagos marina, but it was one of those places that relaxed me.

'Can you order something for me? I'd like to go for a little walk on my own first. I need to stretch my legs.'

'We'll walk with you,' Mum said before Dad pulled her away from me and shook his head.

I heard her tut, and then, as I wandered away, they began to bicker.

Brushing my hand through my newly cropped hair, I smiled. A couple walking towards me, hand in hand, smiled at me. My heart ached at the sight of them, but I continued to smile nonetheless.

Wondering what was happening at home, I sighed. Home. Where was home now? I no longer had one. I was homeless and alone. A single woman; a single woman approaching forty, no less. I hadn't been single since I was seventeen, and it was difficult to digest. What would I do? Where would I go?

Suddenly, my chest felt so constricted that I literally stopped, as if I'd been punched in the stomach. Holding my hand to my chest, a middle-aged woman who had been walking past stopped and moved closer.

'Are you alright, treasure?' she asked in a thick London accent.

'I...I think so,' I answered, looking a little lost.

'I don't reckon you are. You're not having chest pains, are you?'

'No,' I smiled, standing more upright. 'Nothing like that. Don't worry, I'm fine, really. It's more heartache than anything.'

'Oh,' she said sympathetically. 'I remember how that feels. You just have to wait it out, I'm afraid.'

I nodded. 'I know. It's going to be a long wait, I think. My husband has just had a baby with another woman.'

'For goodness' sake,' she said. 'That's terrible. You poor thing, you've got a broken heart, that's what it is.' She looked down at her watch. 'Sugar,' she whispered. 'I'm going to be late. You sure you're alright?'

Raising my eyebrows, I frowned and smiled at the same time. 'I'm sure I'll be fine – eventually. Thank you.'

'Why not stop by my bar for a drink later? On me,' she said, opening her wallet and pulling out a business card before she pointed to the other side of the marina. We're open late. Come on in. We can have a good chat then; if you want to, of course.'

I smiled. 'Thank you. You're very kind. Maybe I will. I'm Eve, by the way,' I said, holding out my hand.

'Diane. Pleased to meet you, Eve. Hopefully, I'll see you later?'

I nodded, and she patted me on the back before rushing off.

'Here she is,' Mum said loudly, as I approached the restaurant where I'd left them. She was eating a small tuna salad while my dad tucked into a burger and chips.

He grinned as I pulled out the chair and sat down. 'I didn't think you'd be wanting any of that bird food rubbish, so I took the liberty of ordering you a burger too.' He winked.

Ordinarily, I'd have preferred a salad, but I was starving, and a burger was exactly what I needed. Tucking in, Mum kept giving me sideways glances and shaking her head.

'I can see you, Mum.'

'What?'

'The disapproving glances you keep giving my hair.'

'Well,' she sighed, dabbing her lips with a napkin. 'You had the most beautiful hair. I can't understand why you would just chop it all off like that. Without even a second's thought. And without talking to me first.'

'You would have only tried to talk me out of it.'

'Of course I would,' she reiterated.

I shook my head and shared a look with Dad. 'Exactly.'

'But why did you do it, love?'

I could feel Dad giving her a nudge under the table, but she ignored it. 'Give it a rest, Joyce,' he said, taking a drink from his mug of steaming tea.

'No, I won't,' she grumbled.

'Mum. It's done. I cut it. That's it. It's gone. And it's my hair, not yours. I'm thirty-nine years old, not bloody thirteen,' I snapped, putting the rest of the burger down. My appetite had disappeared.

She looked away, ashamed; probably ashamed of me, really.

Dad smiled sympathetically and patted me on the hand.

'I understand, love. You're not the first woman to chop off all her hair after a heartbreak. It's perfectly understandable. Just ignore your mother.'

CHAPTER 19

All I remembered was dancing on the bar, and then my mind was completely blank. Opening my eyes, I cringed. Where the hell was I?

Sitting up on the edge of the bed, my stomach did a somersault, and I had to breathe deeply to avoid throwing up. The sound of someone breathing very close gave me palpitations, and when I turned around, I stood up so fast that I had to lean on the wall to stop myself from falling over with dizziness.

Nausea flooded my system, and I rushed through the nearest door, hoping it would lead to a toilet. Luckily it was an en-suite. I closed the door and bent over the bowl, vomiting.

What had happened? Where was I? And more importantly, who the hell was that man?

Grabbing the nearest towel, I put it under my legs and then curled up on the floor, racking my brain, trying to figure out what I'd done.

Incidents flashed in my mind; the bar at the marina, pouring my heart out to Diane, her filling my glass...meeting a group of English women on a hen night and drinking with them. There was another bar then...then, I'd got chatting to a German guy. My hands shot up to my mouth, and I rubbed my face. Everything was shaking, and as the memories flooded back, so did the vomit.

I heaved until there was nothing left.

A gentle tap on the door a few minutes later made me jump. 'Are you okay?' a deep voice asked.

'Y…yes. I'll be fine,' I said quietly.

'I'll make you some coffee,' he said, his footsteps disappearing out of the room.

Counting to ten, I tried to stand, but my legs were so wobbly that I had to lean on the sink for a moment. I splashed my face and opened his cupboard. Taking out the toothpaste, I squeezed a little onto my finger and rubbed it over my teeth before spitting it out and gargling with some water. The simple act of bending my head back made my stomach roll over, and I spat, waiting for it to start convulsing again.

Luckily it didn't, and I just stood looking at myself in the mirror for a minute. I looked like a panda, with my makeup smudged every which way. I needed a shower to wash him off me. I didn't even know him, and I'd ended up in his bed. I felt like some cheap slut, as tears rolled down my face. Who had I become? Who was this woman staring back at me? This wasn't me. This wasn't the woman I wanted to be.

oOo

'ARE YOU SURE THIS IS IT?' he asked as I nodded.

'It's what the map says. Thanks for the lift, Dad,' I said, as we both climbed out of the car. He opened the boot and pulled out my luggage.

'Are you sure you want to do this, love? You know you can stay with us for as long as you need to?'

'I know, Dad. But I just want to be on my own for a bit. I felt really good at Sagres last week, so staying up here on the west coast is just what I need to help myself out. It's quiet too, maybe I'll be able to do a bit of writing.'

'You know your mother's quite upset that you're not going to be with us for your birthday?'

'I know, Dad. But it's my birthday, not hers, and I really need to be alone right now.'

'If you're sure, love?' he asked.

'I'm sure. Oh, this must be them now. I'll ring you,' I said, turning to look at the B&B where I'd be spending the next seven days, before waving Dad off as he drove away.

'Eve Brooke?' said a beautiful Italian woman, in her late thirties, with huge eyes.

Nodding, I held out my hand. 'You must be Flavia. Thank you for accepting the booking at such late notice.'

'Not a problem at all,' she said, as we walked through the gate. An attractive man in his mid-thirties walked towards us with a beaming grin on his face. 'Eve, a pleasure to meet you. I'm Michele! Welcome to Onda Vicentina.'

oOo

As the reviews on the internet had indicated, Onda Vicentina was the perfect B&B for pure relaxation. Not only that but the owners, Michele and Flavia, did everything possible to ensure my comfort and enjoyment during my stay. And when I did want to talk, they were eager to practise their English. It was utter heaven, and it was exactly what I needed to try and decide what I would do with my life.

Matt had sent me an email with the details of the sale of our house – it was going through in less than a week. So sudden, just like most things in my life, lately. But it meant I could do whatever I wanted to do. I just needed to decide what that would be.

During breakfast the following morning, there were a few new guests, eager to surf. Michele, a keen surfer himself, was regaling the group about the wonders of surfing at the local beaches, particularly at a beach called Monte Clerigo, where there was a good surf school. Having never tried it myself, I allowed myself to imagine what it might be like, the freedom of riding on top of the waves with the wind in my hair. Well, in the little hair I had left.

'Why don't you go too, Eve?' asked Michele.

'Oh no, I don't think I'd be much good at it.'

'No? How will you ever know unless you try?' He grinned as he went through to the area where they kept the boards and suits that they rented to keen guests.

'Well, I suppose I won't, but I'm forty years old... in two days.' I smiled, watching as he carried some of them out for the guests to see.

'Wow,' said Flavia, smiling. 'Then you should try something new.'

'And if you wanted to try it, this would be a good board for you,' Michele offered. 'And this suit should fit you.'

'But I really have no idea what to do,' I said, getting a bit nervous.

'You can swim, though?' Flavia asked, as she started clearing the tables.

I nodded.

'Try it. You might enjoy it.' She smiled again. 'You could take a class with the school.'

'Or I can show you the basics, if you don't want to commit to a full class,' offered Stephen, one of the other guests.

Michele laughed. 'Stephen has been surfing for years. He's almost a pro surfer, you'll be in good hands.'

Getting up the courage to try something new, I stood up and stretched. 'Okay, I'll give it a try. But I'll need a lift, I don't have a car.'

'We can take you,' smiled Stephen's girlfriend, Elena. 'It'll be nice to have some female company for a change.'

'Great. Give me five minutes.'

oOo

THERE WAS no doubt about it. I officially sucked at surfing. Stephen and Elena both spent hours trying to get me up on the board, but I was absolutely useless. I failed every single time. It had been fun though, but in the end, I gave up and went and lay on the sand, watching as they wowed with their amazing moves. After a while, they gave up; 'on account of the small waves', they'd said. My cheeks reddened; to me, they were huge!

It was a wonderful day spent in the sun, and it wasn't until we were back at Onda Vicentina and I stood in the shower when I realised I'd gone a whole day without thinking about Adam, or Matt and the baby. It was the first time in ages that I'd let myself enjoy a full day without moping. Was I finally moving on?

Why the hell would you want to move on? Asked the devil on my shoulder. She hadn't shown her face for a while, either. 'Why would I not want to move on?' I whispered, responding to my own imagination.

Because you love him. Why don't you just go back to him? Asked the devil. Because it's too raw. It's too close. He was married to Charlie, the woman who had my husband's baby. It's just too much. I can't bear it. Oh, get over yourself, she said to me again. If you love him, you should be with him.

No, I thought, stepping out of the shower. Besides, he hasn't tried to contact me. He doesn't want me.

That's what it boiled down to. Adam no longer wanted me; that much was obvious. I sat on the bed, wrapped in the towel, and picked up my phone.

'Hey, gorgeous, how are you? How's Portugal?' said the smiley voice on the other end.

'It's good, Lisa. I'm having some valuable me-time. It's just what I need.'

'Then why do you sound so down?' she asked.

I sighed. 'Because I miss him,' I admitted.

'Why don't you call him?' she asked.

'Because I'm not ready and I don't think he is, otherwise he would have called me.'

'He wants to call you, Eve, but he knows you need time on your own.'

'I know.'

'Hey,' she said. 'Don't worry, everything is going to be great. Trust me.'

I laughed. 'I hope you're right.'

'When are you coming home?' she asked.

'Soon. I'll email you.'

'You sure you're okay?' she asked, like a concerned mother.

'I will be.' I smiled. 'How are you?'

'Oh, I'm always good,' she said dismissively. 'Just enjoy yourself. Speak soon, babe.'

CHAPTER 20

After breakfast, I'd taken a long leisurely walk down to the beach, watching the Atlantic Ocean pound against the cliffs. Numerous surfers were demonstrating how easy it was for those in the know. Clearly, I wasn't such a person, and I smiled, eventually sitting down in the soft sand. The sun was a little too warm, so I moved to a shadier spot and just relaxed, watching families making sandcastles while others kicked a football about together. They all seemed so content in this little corner of the Algarvean coast.

A toddler with shoulder-length blonde curly hair carried a ball towards me, holding it out. She grinned at me. I took the ball, and she nodded. I pointed to her family, and she chuckled.

'Do you want me to throw it?' I asked.

She took the ball out of my hands and tried to bounce it on the sand. It just sat there. She stood looking over it, frowning.

Suddenly, a tall man with matching curls appeared. 'Sorry,' he said, taking the little girl's hand in his. 'Come on, Eliza. Stop bothering the nice lady.'

'She's no bother,' I said as they walked away, him kicking the ball at their feet. The girl giggled every time he touched it with his foot.

I smiled and looked away. My heart ached a little bit like it did every time a child paid me some attention. It had been over ten years since I'd found out I would never have children of my own; sometimes it seemed to be getting easier, yet at other times my heart felt like it would break in two, knowing that kids would never be a part of my life. Knowing that nobody would ever call me Mum. I would never be that person that someone relied on over anyone else in the world to raise them.

Before I realised it, I was crying. I sniffled and wiped at the tears in my eyes. Mum, Mother, Ma, Mom, Mama... I would only ever be Eve. It still hurt, but it was a pain that was slowly dissolving. I was forty years old, now; I had to accept what life had dealt me. And that meant that it would only ever be just me. I could live with that, right?

Glancing upwards when a rogue cloud blocked out the sun, I noticed a couple of restaurants and coffee bars beside the beach, so I carefully stood up and made my way over to the nearest one. Looking down at my watch, I noticed it was lunchtime already. The restaurant was getting busier, but I managed to find a table overlooking the beach.

Perusing the menu, I decided on sardines. They were certainly not something I would ordinarily choose, but it was my fortieth birthday, and after I'd tried and failed at surfing, I'd decided today would be the day I would slowly start to change my life. It was the day I would start experimenting a little more, doing things I wouldn't ordinarily do.

So there I was, sitting in a restaurant tucking into a plate of sardines, drinking half a bottle of wine. Alone. But the thing was, I didn't seem to mind. For the first time in a while, I felt content.

oOo

PUSHING open the door to my room, I grinned at the sight of a lovely little cake, a bottle of wine with a single wine glass and a beautiful handmade card wishing me a happy fortieth birthday. 'With very best wishes from your hosts, Michele & Flavia.'

I grinned, flopping onto the bed. The sight of a single wine glass didn't seem to bother me anymore, either. Even though I'd eaten a traditional little custard bun, pastel de nata, at the restaurant, it didn't stop me from tucking into the delicious cake so kindly supplied by the owners of Onda Vicentina. It was such a lovely gesture, and it had certainly helped to make my birthday a special one.

However, I was keen to share the wine with them, so I headed round to the main house, knocking on the door to see if they were still home.

'Flavia?' I asked, knocking again. 'Michele?'

'Happy birthday,' came a shout from within as Michele appeared.

'Hi, Michele. Thank you so much for the cake and wine. It was a lovely surprise,' I said grinning.

'Happy birthday Eve,' yelled Flavia, appearing behind him, wearing a chef's apron. She came outside and hugged me, kissing me on both cheeks. 'Are you having a nice day?' she asked.

I nodded. 'Yes, it's lovely. I've been to the beach, and I've had my first ever sardines.'

'Your first?' asked Michele frowning. 'But your parents live here, right?'

'Yes they do, but I never wanted to try them. I always thought they looked gross.'

'And?' asked Flavia. 'Do you still think so?'

I waited a moment before shaking my head. 'Delicious.'

'See,' Michele said, laughing. 'It's always good to step out of your comfort zone.'

'Actually, I agree. But surfing is definitely still a no-no.'

Michele and Flavia both laughed.

'Thank you for this,' I said, holding up the wine. 'But I'd really like to share it with you. It's not too early for you, is it?'

Michele checked his watch. 'It is a little early...'

'But it is my fortieth birthday,' I pleaded.

Flavia disappeared into the kitchen, returning with three glasses.

'But we would be delighted to drink a glass with you,' Michele finished.

After he had opened the bottle and poured us all a glass of the local wine, we stood up and clinked glasses. 'Salute,' they said loudly.

'Salute, guys, and thank you so much for being such wonderful hosts.'

'You look lovely, dear. It's just such a shame about your ha... well, enough of that. Our guests will be arriving soon, so come on down when you're ready,' Mum said as she closed my bedroom door.

I'd returned from the west coast to discover Mum had organised a party in my honour. To cheer me up, apparently; a belated fortieth birthday party.

Had she done it before I'd gone away, I would have probably refused to attend, but the week-long break had done me a lot of good, and I was ready to face the world again. Straightening my spine, I smiled at myself in the mirror as I stood up, grabbing a cardigan just in case it got chilly out by the pool later. I wore a new dress that I'd purchased from a surf shop in Vila do Bispo, on a day out with Stephen and Elena. It was covered in large yellow and pink flowers and was fitted at the waist and flared out, ending just below the knee. It was completely different from anything I'd ever owned. Matt would have hated it, but I loved it, and that thought made me smile as I turned and walked down the stairs. Dad was busy flitting from the fridge to the barbecue beside the pool, and Mum was busy entertaining the first few guests who had just arrived.

'Ah, here you are, dear,' she said, pulling me towards them. 'You might remember Geoff and Helen. They bought the house next door about a year after us?' she asked.

I nodded and smiled. 'Of course. It's lovely to see you again. How are you?' I asked as Mum left us to chat.

Minutes later, another group arrived, followed by more and more people. Eventually, there were about thirty people all milling about, mingling, drinking, helping Dad cook the meat on the barbie. The weather was perfect, just warm enough but not too overpowering for a day in early May.

It hadn't gone unnoticed that Mum had invited several single men, a couple of whom had clamoured for my attention, competing with each other. But I hadn't been attracted to either one, so I'd merely smiled and gone to help Mum in the kitchen.

'Thanks for this, Mum,' I said, as we took the cling-film off of a couple more salads.

'Are you enjoying yourself, love?'

I stood for a moment, and when I didn't reply, she stopped what she was doing and turned around.

'Love?'

'I was thinking about it... and the answer is yes, I am. It's... nice to just relax and be me. I don't think I've really been myself for a long time.'

'I agree. That...Matt,' she practically spat out his name, 'took that away from you.'

'No, Mum. It was me that took it away from me. It wasn't Matt's fault. I was the other one that let it happen. I allowed myself to become someone else because I wanted to be a good wife, I wanted to please him. For a while, anyway. I guess that all changed in the year before it all went tits up.'

Mum looked at me, disapprovingly. 'Evelyn, that's such a horrible expression.'

'Oh, Mum,' I chuckled. 'You'll never change, will you? I do love that about you, even when you drive me insane sometimes.'

Trying not to laugh, I elbowed her gently in the side and then tickled her.

'Evie,' she suddenly giggled. 'Oh Evie, it's like you're back again. You're really back. I missed you.'

'I missed me too, Mum.'

oOo

Hey honey.

How are you doing? I mean, really doing? You said you'd email! I guess you forgot. I hope spending some time in Portugal is doing you a world of good. I'd love to hear what you've been up to if anything. If not, I want to hear about that too. There's been lots happening here, but I won't bore you with any of that at the moment. We can talk about everything when you're ready. I'm not going to name any names, because I don't want you getting all upset again, but we are missing you. Write soon, honey. Even if it's just a one-liner to say you're okay. Okay?

Big hug from the most dismal May in history.

Lisa xxx

I REREAD IT. 'WE MISS YOU'. 'We miss you'? Who's we? She meant Adam, right? He was really missing me. I hit reply.

Hey Lisa.

Just a quick one. I'm fine. Better than fine, actually. I'm finding myself. All is okay. No need to worry.

I'm coming home.

Miss you too.

Eve xxx

I LAY BACK on the bed and grinned. Something stirred in my stomach, but I pushed it down. I didn't want to think about it yet. I just wanted to continue on my journey to find me. And that would be hurried along by going home and finally being with the man I loved.

CHAPTER 22

I knew he was there the second I stepped foot off the plane; I just felt his presence. Rushing through passport control and impatiently waiting for my luggage to appear on the carousel, I finally ran to the exit. Searching the sea of faces, my eyes eventually stopped on his.

Adam.

He was holding a large bunch of yellow roses, and his face lit up at the sight of me. I left the trolley behind me and ran straight towards him. In my heart, I wanted to kiss him, but my head was stopping me. So I just stood there, swallowing, trying to figure out what to do.

I could tell Adam was feeling the same way. 'Why didn't you call me?' he said.

'Sorry?' I asked.

'You didn't call me. You just got on a plane and buggered off. How was I supposed to feel about that, Eve? Not a word, nothing.'

'Hang on just a minute. You were the one that ran out of the hospital after calling Matt a son of a bitch, then sent your ex-wife round to see me. Not you? Not the day later. Nothing, Adam. You left me to pick up the pieces.'

'No, Eve. It wasn't like that. This is so messed up.'

'Too right it's messed... no, it's fucked up. That's what this is,' I cried, not understanding what was happening any more. Didn't he want me? But he brought roses.

'Eve, don't,' he whispered, reaching out to me.

I turned to look at him, and in that instant, I saw it. The hurt. The hurt that I had showered on him and I crumbled. He caught me and pulled me close.

'Oh Eve, we both messed this up, didn't we? I thought you wanted to get away from me. I was giving you space, but when you didn't try to reach out to me, I figured you wanted nothing to do with me. Oh, Eve. You thought the same thing, didn't you?'

I nodded and looked up into his eyes.

'Don't you get it?'

I searched his eyes. 'Get what?' I whispered.

'I love you, Eve. I always have.'

'You do?'

He nodded.

'But what about Charlie?'

'You're asking me about Charlie? She's in love with Matt. Matt's in love with Charlie. They're both in love, with baby Eviemay and I'm in love with you.'

'Eviemay?' I cringed.

'Yes, it's a little creepy, right?' He laughed.

I nodded as he pulled me up into his arms.

'Eve, why did you run away?'

'I was so hurt, Adam.'

'Because of the baby?'

I nodded silently.

Adam stroked my cheek. 'Oh, babe. You should have run to me, not away from me. I can help soothe that hurt,' he said, placing his hand lovingly over my heart.

'But you were so angry. The way you stormed out of the hospital, like that... I thought you must have still loved Charlie a little bit.'

'Eve, don't you understand? I was so angry because if they'd come clean right at the beginning, we could have been together from the start. We wouldn't have had to fight it all that time. It could have been me and you months earlier. I was angry because they let me believe it was my baby. I thought I had to do the right thing because of my baby, but it wasn't my baby, was it? I thought I could never be with you again, but I could... They lied, and that's what pissed me off. You're all I care about now.'

'And your kids.' I smiled.

'Well, yes, the kids too.'

'I'm sorry, Adam.'

'I'm sorry too, Eve.'

oOo

'WHAT'S BOTHERING YOU, EVE?' Adam asked, in the car, a little while later.

'What makes you think something's bothering me?'

He shrugged. 'Isn't there?'

He was right, of course. Something was worrying me. 'I'm homeless, Adam. I don't have a base to go back to. I don't know what to do. Should I go to a hotel for a while? I just don't know.'

'Eve, you certainly won't go to a hotel. I'd just assumed you would move in with me.'

I looked up at him in shock. 'You had?'

'Of course. I assumed that's what you wanted. I know it's what I want. I'm sorry... was I wrong? I can set up different accommodations if that makes you feel more comfortable?'

Those butterflies in my tummy started fluttering around like crazy again, and I grinned. 'Oh my God, Adam, really? Of course, that's what I'd like. I'd love to. Yes, yes,' I said, almost jumping out of my seat. 'I'm the happiest woman in the world, right now. But it will be a bit weird.'

'What will be?' he asked.

'Living in a house that also belonged to Charlie and seeing someone else living in my old house.'

'Oh no,' Adam said. 'Didn't I tell you?'

'Tell me what?'

'I signed the deeds of that place over to Charlie. When I asked you to move in with me, I meant for you to live with me at the manor.'

'Holy shit,' I muttered. 'Nothing would make me happier. Will we go straight there from the airport?'

'Unless you want to go somewhere else?'

I shook my head. There was only one thing on my mind, and my cheeks flushed red. 'I want to finish what we started... in the pool,' I whispered into his ear.

He grinned and then took my hand, placing it ever so carefully in his crotch. 'I think this proves I want that too, Eve,' he said wickedly.

Holy crap. Electricity shot out from my stomach and crept slowly downwards until the heat started to throb right where it mattered.

I couldn't wait to get there.

oOo

I woke up the next morning to the delicious aroma of bacon floating up from the kitchen. For a split second, I was confused, and then, when the wonderful memories came flooding back, I grinned and jumped out of bed. Grabbing my dressing gown from the floor, I ran downstairs.

'Hey sexy,' breathed the most erotic voice I've ever heard. Adam stood in the kitchen, preparing breakfast.

'You're cooking breakfast for me?' I asked, rushing towards him.

He nodded and picked me up by my bottom, placing me carefully on the worktop. 'I am. I hope you're hungry.'

'Ooh yes, I'm always hungry,' I replied as seductively as possible.

He grinned and pulled me close, kissing every part of my face and neck.

'God, you smell so good,' he murmured, before turning off the bacon and carrying me back up to the bedroom for a repeat performance of the night before.

An hour later, we were back in the kitchen, famished. Adam prepared bacon, eggs, sausages and toast while I simply made the coffee and poured some orange juice. He whistled as he worked, and I couldn't wipe the grin off my face. I was in heaven. It had been such a long time coming, but here it was. I'd never felt so good, and boy was it amazing.

The sound of a buzzing noise broke me out of my reverie, and I realised it was Adam's phone. He walked over to it and clicked on the text message.

'Is everything all right?' I asked.

'Let's just eat breakfast, and I'll tell you...'

'Tell me what?'

'What's been going on.'

'That sounds ominous.'

He placed all the food on our plates and carried them to the table, where we sat down.

'So what's up, Adam? What's going on?'

'One of the reasons I was unable to come and find you in Portugal...' He stopped and took a gulp of orange juice.

'Yes?'

'It was because of Amy.'

'Amy? What happened to Amy? Is she okay, Adam?'

He looked away and shook his head. 'She's...she's... pregnant.'

'Oh,' I said, smiling. 'Well that's wonderful, isn't it? Or are you frightened of becoming a grandfather?' I teased. 'Or don't you like the father?'

The look on his face made my smile drop. 'What?'

'The baby's father. He's... he's...not really in the picture.'

'Oh, that's a shame.'

Adam shook his head, 'It's not that. It's, erm, it's Amy. She came out.'

'She came out of where?' I asked innocently.

'No, Eve. She came out,' he reiterated.

'You mean she's...she's gay?' I asked tentatively.

Adam slowly nodded, taking a swig of orange juice.

'Oh Adam, you look like you need something stronger than orange juice.' I smiled. 'She's gay. So what? What's the problem? If she's happy, that's all that matters. Is she having a baby with her girlfriend, then? Are they together?'

Adam nodded. 'Clare. I've known her for years. They've been best friends since they were thirteen.'

'Have they been, erm, together since then?'

'Apparently,' Adam said, through gritted teeth.

'Are you not okay with this?' I asked.

'She's my daughter, Eve. How can I be okay with it?'

'Because she's your daughter, Adam. That's exactly the reason you should be okay with it. Do you love your daughter?'

'Of course I do. She means the world to me.'

I smiled. 'Which would suggest that her happiness means the world to you too, right?'

Adam smiled. 'You're so smart, aren't you?'

'You're not the first person to tell me that,' I said, tucking into my breakfast, before adding, 'there I was, worried sick that there was something wrong with her. How has Lisa taken it?' I asked.

Adam snorted. 'Apparently, Amy confided in Lisa a few years ago.'

'Ouch,' I said.

'I know, that's what hurt the most. That and the fact that...'

'What?'

'Amy didn't want to tell me because she knew I was going through something deeply upsetting myself.'

'Aww, I'd love to meet her. She sounds like a wonderful girl.'

Smiling, Adam nodded. 'Oh, she is.'

'How did she know you were going through something?'

'Do you really want to know?'

I raised my eyebrows.

'Jack told her about his encounter with us here.'

'Oh.'

'Exactly.'

'What did they say when you told them what happened?' I asked as I finished eating, putting my knife and fork down.

'Actually, they weren't surprised. Amy used some pretty foul language to describe Charlie and said I should go and find you immediately.'

'Really?' I asked as I felt my eyes well up with tears. 'She wants us to be together?'

'It certainly seems that way,' he said, pushing his chair back and dragging me out of my seat and onto his lap. 'She wants her father to be happy, and Lisa told her only one person could make me the happiest man on Earth.'

'Oh, really? And who might that be?' I asked inquisitively.

His mouth on mine answered that question.

CHAPTER 23

We'd started taking daily walks, some out in the countryside, others in the city or through local villages. It had become something to really look forward to. Not only were we getting to spend some real quality time together, but we were also getting to see more of our beautiful country. After spending a little bit of time in Portugal, I vowed to start enjoying more of what the world has to offer, and I wanted to start with what was on our doorstep.

That afternoon we were ambling along the cliff tops in the north of Somerset.

'Eve?' Adam suddenly whispered quietly, under his breath.

I dragged my eyes away from the sea view. 'Yeah?' I asked. 'What's up?'

Droplets of water began to fall from the sky, and I looked up; dark grey clouds were moving quicker than I'd anticipated. 'Ooh. Looks like a storm's coming,' I said absent-mindedly.

'As I was saying,' Adam said, clearing his throat.

The rain began to come down heavier.

'Adam, we're getting soaked. We'd better go back to the car.'

'Eve, I'm trying to...'

I turned back to him, and he was crouching down on one knee. 'Adam?' I asked, my heart fluttering in my chest. 'Oh,' I put my hands over my mouth and squealed as he pulled out a little box from his pocket. All the while, the rain poured down in buckets.

'Evelyn. Will you do me the honour of becoming my wife?'

'Holy crap,' I yelled. 'Yes! Yes! Yes!' I answered as he stood up and pulled me into a long hug.

'The ring, the ring?' I said, eager to get a good look.

Adam laughed and stepped backwards. He opened the box and handed it to me.

'Oh, Adam, it's exquisite. It must have cost a fortune,' I chuckled, putting it on my finger. It fitted perfectly, the solitary diamond twinkling even without the sunlight to dance on it.

'Adam, I'm so happy. I love you so much.'

'I love you too, Eve,' he said, putting the empty box back in his pocket before he picked me up and twirled me around in the rain, then he put me down and dipped me before he started singing.

We danced together in the rain, Adam's voice crooning the lyrics of Singing in the Rain instead of Gene Kelly's, and I felt as though my heart might burst with love for him.

I laughed, watching as he did his little dance routine before we ran back to the car. We fell inside laughing. Eventually, we sat, quietly looking at each other. Our breathing had caused the windows to fog up.

He leaned forward and kissed me gently on the lips. A kiss that deepened until his hands were all over me, inside my blouse, unclasping the bra so that my breasts fell into his palms. He bent forward and took a nipple into his mouth, gently toying with it with his teeth. I groaned and moved my hands over him until they reached his hardness, tight against his jeans. Groans of delight echoed through the car while I carefully removed my jeans and panties and then straddled him. It wasn't easy, but the passion was too much to stop and head home. I needed him. He needed me. Simple as that.

CHAPTER 24

*I*t was surreal waking up with a grin on my face every day. I had become so accustomed to dreading the day ahead and what kind of mood Matt would be in when I woke. But now, Adam was always there with me, always smiling. Always loving. I had fallen deeply in love, and it felt amazing. I should've known stormy seas lay ahead. I should have expected it. Life that sweet couldn't really last could it?

We were awoken by the sound of the phone ringing. Turning to look at the bedside clock, we panicked. It was half-past two in the morning, and that was never a good sign.

'What's going on?' I moaned, rubbing my eyes.

'The phone,' he said, jumping out of bed at breakneck speed and rustling through the jeans he'd been wearing the day before. 'My mobile,' he muttered.

'Amy?' he said, trying to sound calm. 'What's the matter?'

He sat down on the edge of the bed, and I inched closer, putting my hands on his shoulders. I could feel his muscles tensing.

'Oh, God. I'll be right there,' he turned to look at me and corrected himself immediately. 'We'll be right there.' He threw the phone on to the bed and began quickly dressing. 'It's Lisa. We need to get to the hospital right away.'

'What's wrong? What's happened?' I cried, moving deftly to the wardrobe to grab my jeans and a jumper.

'They're not sure yet. She was complaining of pain, and then she collapsed. An ambulance took her to the hospital,' he said, his eyes welling with tears.

'Oh, God, Adam. Don't worry. She's in good hands over there.'

He nodded and ran out of the room, and I followed him the second I had my clothes on.

oOo

IT WAS the smell that got to me again, illness combined with intensive cleaning products. Having rushed out of the house without drinking anything, my stomach rolled over with nausea. But perhaps it wasn't just that; it was the memory of the last time I stepped through those doors. I tried to block it from my mind. I was happy. I didn't need reminding of that awful betrayal.

'Lisa Grove, please,' said Adam to the nurse on reception.

'I'm sorry?' she asked as she checked the monitor and shook her head. 'Nobody by that name has been admitted.'

Adam shook his head. 'No, sorry, not Grove. Lisa Oakwood.'

'Yes, of course,' she said, pointing to the screen. 'She's having some tests done at the moment. If you head on up to the waiting room on the third floor, the doctors will let you know as soon as they can.'

Adam nodded and turned to walk away. I tried to keep up.

When we reached the third-floor waiting room, a stunning young woman with a mass of dark curls rushed towards us.

'Daddy,' she cried.

Adam opened his arms wide and pulled her to him. 'Amy, sweetheart. Are you alright?' he asked, as she sobbed.

She shook her head. 'It was awful, Dad. She came into our room c...c-complaining of p-p-pain, and then she just c-c-collapsed.'

I stood helplessly beside them, as he rubbed her back tenderly.

'Don't worry, she's in the best place, right now. She's being looked after here. We just have to be patient for a while, okay?' he asked, drawing away from her so he could see her face.

146

Her eyes were red and swollen.

I watched as his own lips trembled, and he pulled her back towards him.

A pretty girl with short blonde hair, about the same age as Amy, was standing a few feet in front of us. She was twisting a lovely green cotton scarf around her fingers. I smiled and stepped towards her. 'You must be Clare,' I said quietly.

She nodded. 'And you're Eve?'

I nodded, and we both smiled.

'Shall we go and get some coffee for everyone?' I asked, turning and noticing Amy's slightly protruding pregnant belly. 'Or tea?'

Clare let out a deep sigh and nodded. 'I think that's a good idea.'

I rubbed Adam's arm as we walked past them and went to find the nearest cafe or drinks machine.

'I think there's a cafeteria down there,' Clare said sadly.

'Yes, I think so. Are you alright?' I asked.

She nodded and then shook her head. 'No, not really. It was a bit scary, the ambulance coming and everything. I thought she was going to die. Amy was hysterical.'

'I'm sure she was,' I said as we arrived in a small cafeteria, where the lights were off. 'Looks closed.'

'There's a machine though.' She pointed further down the corridor. 'But I don't want to go back yet, not just yet.'

'I understand. Let's sit for a minute, shall we?'

Clare looked at me gratefully and nodded as we approached a row of four seats. Sitting down, I said nothing for a while, thinking Clare probably needed to process whatever it was that was happening, but she spoke up first. 'I think Lisa might have been ill for a while, Eve.'

I looked up, surprised. 'You do? Why do you think that?'

She shrugged. 'I have this thing.'

'Thing?' I asked, intrigued.

She blushed. 'Her aura was changing colour.'

'Oh. You can see people's auras?'

She nodded slowly. 'I don't tell many people, because they think I'm nuts.'

'I don't think you're nuts.'

She looked at me with wide, watery eyes. 'It's my fault,' she whispered.

'What do you mean, it's your fault?'

Clare broke down in tears. 'I saw her aura changing, and I didn't tell anyone. I should have said something earlier. I could have prevented this from happening,' she gushed.

'Oh Clare,' I said, putting my arm around her shoulders. 'It's not your fault at all. Don't blame yourself. You weren't to know this would happen. Besides, she's in the best possible place right now, isn't she?'

Clare sniffed and nodded. 'I noticed it was different yesterday, and I didn't say anything.'

'Only yesterday?' I asked.

She nodded at me. 'I haven't seen her for a few months, so we drove up from Bournemouth to visit.'

'Then you really couldn't have done anything about it. Please don't blame yourself, sweetie. Amy needs you to be strong for her right now. Can you do that?'

Clare sat upright and nodded, wiping her eyes. 'You're right,' she said.

'Do you want to wait a few more minutes before we go back?' I asked.

Clare shook her head, standing up. 'No, let's go and see if they're okay. Oh, I almost forgot the coffee.'

'Don't worry. I hadn't. I'm desperate for one.' I smiled.

Clare smiled back at me. 'I know now why Adam's aura has changed too.'

'It has?' I asked as I pressed the buttons for a cup of coffee.

'Oh yes, most definitely. It's brighter than it has been for a long time,' she said, as I handed her two of the coffees so I could get a third, followed by a cup of tea for Amy.

oOo

THERE WAS little to do but wait for news, so we sat, occasionally dropping off to sleep for a few minutes before some noise or other woke us.

Amy sat beside Adam; they held on to each other's hands tightly. Clare sat beside Amy, holding her other hand, and I sat away from them all, feeling like I was in the wrong place at the wrong time. Somehow I felt like I didn't belong there, like a mistress or something. Why I was feeling guilty, I had no idea. Standing up, I walked past them all. Nobody said a word.

I needed some fresh air, so I walked back through the hospital, down several flights of stairs and out into the morning sunlight. I blinked several times slowly, adjusting to the natural brightness after the fluorescence of the hospital, and went and sat on a bench near the entrance.

Breathing deeply, I shivered and wrapped my arms around myself, wishing that this wasn't happening. That we were still tucked up in bed because Lisa was in perfect health. But that wasn't the case, was it? She'd collapsed. I hoped that it was something easily fixed. Lisa had become my friend; she was one of the most wonderful people I'd ever met, and we'd had so much fun together lately. But she was Amy and Jack's mother. They needed her. And Adam needed her too.

His kids didn't even know me, on the other hand; Adam and I had only been together a few months and hadn't had the chance to meet them yet. It was crazy but they'd just been too busy, and then when they were able to visit, I had to go and do several book signings around the country.

I sighed and looked across the parking lot as several cars came and went. I shivered and was about to stand up when I saw a familiar face in the distance. I recognised it from the photos around the house. He was running through the car park, his face registering shock.

'Jack!' I yelled, but he carried on as if he hadn't heard me. 'Jack!' I shouted even louder.

He turned his head and slowed down before turning and walking quickly towards me. 'Eve?' he asked, and I nodded.

'I'm sorry we have to meet under such horrible circumstances.'

He nodded. 'Yes, I know. Is there any news yet? Is she alright? Where's Dad and Amy?'

'We're still waiting. Your dad hasn't seen her yet. Come on, I'll take you to them.'

'Thanks,' he mumbled.

We walked quickly, neither of us saying anything until I led him into the third-floor waiting room.

'Dad,' he sighed, rushing towards his father, who opened his eyes and released Amy's hand as they both stood up. All three of them hugged.

'Mr Oakwood,' came a voice from behind them.

'Yes,' Adam replied, neglecting to correct the doctor. 'How is she? Is she okay?'

The doctor said, 'She's comfortable. Would you like to come with me?'

Adam nodded and disappeared.

Amy and Jack looked at each other. 'What about us?' Amy said after they'd gone.

'Don't worry, hon,' said Clare. 'I'm sure you'll be able to go and see her afterwards.'

I sighed and sat down, thinking about what the doctor had just said. She's comfortable. Wasn't that what they said when someone was close to death? I gulped and tried not to think about it as I watched the three youngsters in front of me.

Please don't take her.

CHAPTER 25

I placed the cup of hot chocolate in Lisa's hand and made sure she was warm enough. 'How is it?' I asked, sitting down on the soft rug near the fire.

She took a sip and smiled. 'Absolutely yummy. You really do have a knack for making hot chocolate, Evie.'

'Yes, my dad always used to tell me that. You want to know the secret?'

She nodded.

'A little cream and a touch of grated dark chocolate. It makes all the difference.'

'It certainly does.'

'How are you feeling? And be honest. No tiptoeing around me. Adam and the kids are out, so tell me the truth.'

Lisa leaned back in the armchair, and I tried so hard not to show my grimace. She looked deathly pale; her skin had lost its glow, and her eyes looked tired. And then there was her weight – there was very little left of her. But regardless of all that, she hadn't lost her sense of humour.

'Oh, I'm perfectly well. Can't you tell? I look like a catwalk model for the first time in my life.'

I sighed and shook my head. 'Oh, Lisa, it's alright. Tell me.'

She rolled her eyes and took a little sip before handing me the mug. 'I can't manage any more.'

151

I took it from her skinny fingers and placed it on the coffee table. She'd barely touched it.

'I'm comfortable enough. Stop worrying about me.'

Raising my eyebrows, I took a sip of my coffee. 'Lisa, you've got cancer. Of course, I'm going to worry about you.'

'Oh please don't use the C word. It's like a curse word or something.'

'I know. I'm sorry, hon. I just want to make sure you're as comfortable and as pain-free as possible.'

'I know, and you're doing a fabulous job. You're such a good friend, Evie. But...'

'What is it?' I asked, turning the gas up a little after noticing her shiver. There wasn't enough flesh on her bones to keep her warm.

'You know I'm dying.'

'Lisa, no, don't say that,' I cried.

'But it's true. I've accepted it, and now I need you to accept it, and more importantly, I need you to help Amy, Jack and Adam to accept it too. Can you do that? Can you do that for me, Evie?'

I swallowed back the tears and bit my bottom lip, turning away from her for a moment to gather myself before nodding slowly.

'Good, I knew I could count on you. I'm so lucky to have you as my friend, Evie.'

'No, Lisa. I'm the lucky one.'

'Oh don't get all soppy on me now.' She smiled, and her eyelids began to get visibly heavier. 'I'm a little tired. I think I'll take a nap,' she whispered.

I stood up. 'Do you want me to help you to bed?'

'No, I'll sleep right here, in front of the fire, thank you,' she said, as I stood up and readjusted the throw over her lap.

I tiptoed out of the room and closed the door behind me.

e'd rented a house by the sea in Devon; it had been Lisa's idea. She said that's where she'd like to spend her final moments, so we'd pulled out all the stops and found the perfect place with its own little beach. It meant she could sit with her toes in the sand and watch the waves crash against the shore. It was there that she was at her happiest, as life slowly dwindled from her weakening body.

It wasn't easy. Jack was friendly and polite to me, but I knew, deep down, he'd rather I wasn't there. But I hid my emotions; Lisa didn't need to see them. All I cared about was helping her to have the best final few months of her life. Nothing else really mattered.

Hearing movement in the kitchen, I walked towards it before the sounds of people talking loudly slowed me down.

'I'm just so angry with her,' Jack said, slamming a cupboard door.

'I know. I'm angry too,' Adam said.

'You can't be angry with her. It's not Mum's fault she got cancer,' said Amy.

'It's her fault she didn't have chemo, sis,' Jack shouted, choking up. 'The chemo could've healed her.'

'No, Jack. The chemo would just kill her sooner. She wants to die in peace. Can't you understand that? She just wants to go peacefully, with us around her. She doesn't want to get all fucking shot up with all that shit. Just let her be, Jack. Just let her be. All she needs right now is for us to love her and stand beside her while she does what she wants to do.' Amy's voice was quiet but angry.

'You're just gonna let her die and be happy about it?' Jack replied, angrily.

'No, of course not, but what I do want is for her to know that I accept her decision. And you should too.'

'I can't accept her choice to die, Amy.'

'Stop it, both of you. Just stop it,' said Adam's voice, equally as broken. 'This is your mother. My wife.'

I gasped. What the hell happened to ex-wife? I stepped closer to listen.

'I love her so much. Just like you do. And I sure as hell don't want her to die. And yes, I'm angry with her for not fighting. I'm fucking furious, but I will not let her see that. And neither will you, Jack.

'You love her, Dad? Really? Then why did you leave her? You should have stayed with her. We could have stayed together as a family.'

Something smashed on the kitchen floor, and I jumped back.

'I...I...didn't leave her. It was a mutual decision. We shouldn't have been together then. Both of us knew that.'

'Yes, back then you probably shouldn't, but you've grown so close over the past couple of years. And now...I know you still love her. I can see it. You should be with her now, Dad,' Jack said quietly. 'Not with Eve.'

I heard sobs. Adam was sobbing.

I so wanted to walk in and soothe his pain, but something was stopping me. What if Jack was right? What if what Lisa needed right now was a husband? Her husband? And what if that was what Adam needed too?

An involuntarily sob escaped my lips, and I stepped backwards. Turning, I picked up my handbag, car keys and calmly opened the front door. Then I got in my car and drove.

CHAPTER 27

My mobile kept ringing, but I just turned up the music and pressed my foot down on the accelerator, speeding along the motorway. I had no idea where I was going, I just needed to get away for a bit. Just a little bit. Some fresh air. Maybe the beach.

Taking off my shoes, I wiggled my toes in the sand and began walking along the beach at Plymouth Hoe. There were a few people about, even though it wasn't a particularly warm day and grey clouds hovered above. But I ignored everyone, focusing instead on my inner emotions. They were up and down, driving me insane. I was so in love with Adam, and as far as I knew, he felt the same about me. But did he really? Was I just a cover for his true feelings for Lisa? Was he really in love with his first wife? And even if he was, what could I do? She was so close to death, and I'd promised to be there for her. I'd promised to look after her family. How could I do that when I had this sinking feeling that she and Adam were still in love? How could I stick around and be witness to that? My heart was breaking. It had happened before, and it was happening again.

I stood, picking up a couple of pebbles at the same time. Then one by one, I threw them into the sea before I carried on walking along the beach, listening to the sound of the seagulls. An elderly couple sat on a bench, eating chips and smiling at each other. To see love at that age always tugged at my heart, but today it just made it feel like it was bleeding.

I wrapped my cardigan around my body and walked forcefully against the wind, which was picking up. Tears stung my eyes. I turned around and my hair, now a little longer, whipped at my face. My handbag started buzzing again. I opened it and pulled out my phone. I just stared at it until it stopped ringing.

Six missed calls. I clicked on them. Five from Adam. One from my mum. Three text messages from Adam.

WHERE R U? x

WHAT HAPPENED? You just left? X

R U OK? X

I STARTED to text back when it rang again. I sighed and answered it, trying to find somewhere out of the wind.

'Hello?'

'Babe, what happened? I saw you drive off without saying anything? I've been worried sick. Where are you?'

'Paignton,' I replied.

'Paignton? What on Earth are you doing over there?'

I shrugged, knowing he couldn't see me.

'Evie, what's going on? What's wrong?'

'I heard you, Adam. I heard you talking to the kids in the kitchen.'

He was silent for a while. 'But why leave? I don't understand?'

'Didn't you hear me? I said, I heard your conversation. You're still in love with Lisa. Your wife. Not your ex-wife. Your wife. You said you still love her. How can I compete? How can I, Adam? Look, I'm gonna go.'

'No, Eve. Wait. Just... let me meet you somewhere. I'm coming.

Meet me at the pier,' and he rang off before I could say no. I cursed under my breath and went to get a hot drink somewhere while I waited for him to drive over.

oOo

I saw him in the distance, walking towards me. He was so handsome. My stomach somersaulted, and I gulped. I had no idea what I was doing. Was I losing it? Was I seeing things that weren't there? Well, I was an author, after all. My imagination did have a tendency to overreact and imagine things that weren't real.

'Eve,' he said as he approached me, pulling me into his arms. 'What's going on in there?' he asked, tapping the side of my head.

'Oh, Adam, I heard you. You're still in love with her,' I said, pulling away.

'She's dying, Eve. Dying,' he whispered.

'But that's not the point. How can I be with you when I know you love someone else?'

'No, Eve. I don't...'

'Don't what, Adam? Don't love her? Then you're lying to me, or you're lying to your kids, and I know you don't lie to your kids. Do you?'

He sighed and leaned over the railing. 'I do love her, Eve. I stopped loving her for a while, but then I started again. But it's not like you think. It's not like you and me.'

'You and me?'

'We have passion, Eve. Mad, passionate love. It's different with Lisa.'

My heart was literally breaking in my chest. He loved me, but he loved her too. I shook my head. 'I can't take this. I can't.'

He stood up and grabbed hold of my arms. 'Eve, please. She's dying. She's going to die soon,' he said, tears in his eyes. 'Don't leave me. I need you.'

'I can't be your back-up wife, Adam,' I said and walked away from him.

'No,' he yelled. 'It's not like that. Eve, I love you. I've loved you for the past three, four years. Ever since London. Please, don't walk away now.'

I stopped and turned as he ran towards me.

'Just before I met you, I thought I was falling back in love with her, but she was with another man then, and she encouraged me to get married. That's when I married Charlie because I never thought I'd find you. Lisa has always been there for me, Eve. She encouraged me to fight for you.'

I looked into his eyes, confused. 'You fought for me, but were still in love with her?'

'No, oh God, this is coming out all wrong. I loved her for so many reasons, and I still do, of course. She's the mother of my children.'

'Adam, are you in love with her?'

'I...I...don't know.'

I stepped backwards. 'Are you in love with me?' I asked, waiting, closing my eyes.

'Yes,' he said, and I opened them up again. 'I want you. I want to be with you for the rest of my life. But please, for the rest of hers, please come back. She needs you, I need you, the kids need you.'

'The kids?'

He nodded. 'They might not realise it now, but they do. Please, Eve. Please come home with me.'

I turned to watch the crashing waves below, letting everything sink in. There was a possibility that he was in love with Lisa, but he was sure he was in love with me. Could I cope with that? Could I live in a house with a dying woman who was also the object of his love? Could I? I sighed and nodded. I had no choice. It wasn't Lisa's fault, and she was dying. I needed to be there for her. As for Adam? Well, that would take time for me to come to terms with. But for now, all that mattered was Lisa.

CHAPTER 28

'Adam? Adam?' I asked, poking him in the side as I shook my head in distress. 'Wake up. This has got to stop,' I said as he slowly opened his eyes. He was slumped over the kitchen table, an empty bottle of brandy in front of him.

'Adam? I don't know how much more I can take.'

'What?' he asked, rubbing his head. 'Oh,' he groaned.

'Exactly. How long is this going to go on for? Do you really think this is what Lisa wants during her last few days of life? Do you really think she wants you drinking away the days and collapsing every night in a drunken stupor? No, she doesn't. Don't do this to her, Adam. Don't do this to me.'

'You don't know what you're talking about,' he said, standing up and walking over to the sink where he turned the tap on and splashed his face before he grabbed the box of painkillers that he'd been keeping on the work surface for the past few weeks.

'Adam, please. Look at yourself.'

He looked away from me and left the room. Closing my eyes for a second, I sighed heavily before opening them and throwing the brandy bottle into the recycling bin.

'Eve,' shouted a tired voice from the hallway.

'What's up, Clare?' I asked, walking towards her.

Immediately I knew something was wrong. 'Clare? What is it?'

Tears rolled down her cheeks, and she nodded. 'You need to get Adam. It's time.'

'No, no, no,' I whispered, rushing back through the kitchen, desperately searching for him. 'Adam, Adam, you need to come quickly. Babe!' I shouted. 'Babe?'

He appeared by the back door, looking like death. 'What is it?'

'It's Lisa,' I said, holding out my hand.

He ignored it, the blood draining from his face, as he rushed passed me and bounded through the house, into her room.

'Amy, my beautiful girl,' Lisa croaked from the bed in the downstairs room with a perfect view of the sea.

'Mum,' Amy sobbed as she carefully sat on the bed, holding her mother's weak fingers, careful not to break the skin, skin that had become like tissue paper. It was difficult for the young woman to sit comfortably with a huge bump in front of her.

'Amy,' Lisa whispered. 'I love you so much, my darling. I wish I could have met your baby.' She stopped and sobbed. 'You're going to make the most amazing mother. And so is Clare,' she smiled. 'My girls. Clare?' she said a little louder.

Clare stepped forward, tears pouring down her face.

'Look after each other. You're my girls. Be kind to one another, stay in love forever and ever.'

Clare nodded, squeezing Amy's shoulder.

'Mum?' said Amy. 'We're going to call her Lisa, our baby. Lisa.'

Lisa smiled, her eyes welling up even more. 'That makes me so very happy, my darling. Thank you. I'm sorry we'll just miss meeting each other, but I'll be here, watching over you, I promise. Jack?'

The girls stood up, Amy leaning over to kiss her mother, before moving away so Jack could step forward and sit down.

'Mum?' he said. 'I wish you'd have fought more, you know?'

Lisa nodded, whispering ever so slowly, 'I know, honey. I know. But it's my time. I know that. I knew it all along. You be strong, okay? Find a lovely woman to love. You deserve all the love in the world, my darling. I love you so much. Be strong, be brave and be happy, Jack. I'll always be here,' she tried to lift her hand but failed. 'In your heart.' She coughed.

'Mum, I love you. I'll miss you so much,' he sobbed, letting his head drop to her side.

'I know, but I'll be here, always. Adam?'

Jack slowly stood up, wiping away his tears as his father cleared his throat and walked towards the woman who had borne his children over twenty years ago.

'Honey?' Lisa whispered. 'Thank you for bringing joy to my life. I always loved you, you know that right?' she croaked, and he nodded, wiping the tears roughly from his cheeks.

'I want you to be happier than you've ever been, you hear me?' she smiled. 'That woman,' she lifted her finger just slightly and pointed to me. 'Evie, she's your soul mate. Did you know that? I knew all along.' Her voice became weaker. 'Be happy. Be good together. She loves you so much. Be happy together forever.'

Adam didn't even look at me, he just wiped his eyes and leaned forward to kiss her hollow cheek.

'Kids,' she whispered. They all stepped forward. 'Be understanding. Your father and Evie, they are perfect for each other. I want you to both accept it for what it is. True love.'

Amy let out a deep cry, and Jack sobbed.

'Evie, my friend. Thank you,' was all she said before she closed her eyes.

The nurse stepped forward. 'I'm sorry, she doesn't have long left now.'

'Mum,' they cried, rushing to her side and kneeling on the floor.

There they sat for half an hour, nobody saying a thing. We just watched as the life slowly left her, her breathing finally ceasing.

'Mum, don't go. Don't leave us,' Amy sobbed.

Jack put his arm across her shoulder. 'She's gone, Amy. She's gone. '

A deep guttural groan echoed throughout the room, and Amy gasped. 'Oh, God, the baby. The baby. She's coming. She's coming now.'

'Oh shit,' said Adam, as I rushed toward her and helped her up.

'Hospital. We need to get to the hospital now,' I said.

'No,' Amy said, searching my face and then looking back at her mother who was now, finally, at peace. 'Here, I want to have the baby here. I need to. I know it sounds crazy, but I need to have this baby right now, in this house.'

Lisa's nurse did everything possible while we waited for a midwife to come from the local hospital.

Baby Lisa was born just a couple of hours after her grandmother passed away. Once I knew Amy and the baby were okay, I left.

CHAPTER 29

The second I had arrived at the airport, I had scanned the departures leaving that day and booked the first flight that appealed to me. Canada.

I'd flown into Calgary, hired a car with GPS and then driven straight to Banff, where I'd managed to book an apartment online while at the airport. En-route I had to buy a park pass, which I hadn't been expecting but the idea of staying in a Canadian National Park just made me smile. Matt would have hated it. He was all about holidays in the sun where the weather was as warm as it could possibly be. I had tolerated it because I'd wanted Matt to be happy. If I wanted to make myself happy, then this was where I would have come.

Adam, on the other hand; I didn't have a clue. He'd let me in for such a short time, and then he'd pushed me away. I felt like I'd lost him all over again. I'd lost him even before I'd lost Lisa. He'd assured me I was the one he wanted, but then he'd hit the bottle and completely shut me out. A couple of tears fell down my cheeks, and I sniffed loudly, wiping them away.

I had to try and forget him, regardless of what Lisa had said before she died. It was clear that he was too hung up on his ex-wife, even now that she'd gone; all he wanted to do was drown his sorrows. We were over, and I had to accept that. That's why I'd run away, again. I needed to be completed alone. To find myself. To really find myself, this time.

Pulling up outside what appeared to my little apartment block, I found a spot to park my big Canadian car and then headed up the stairs, where I was greeted by a lovely lady who handed me the key and told me everything I needed to know.

Afterwards, I dropped my luggage on the sofa, walking through to look at the tiny kitchen. It was perfect for me. Through the kitchen was a bedroom with another window that looked out onto a pretty little courtyard. A simple yet fully functional bathroom was located next door.

I flopped onto the bed and closed my eyes, sighing. I was so lost, and I was hoping running away would help me find myself again. Tears poured down my cheeks, and I spent the rest of the evening crying.

Once I'd run out of tears, I decided enough was enough, so the next day I explored the town, making small talk with the locals, finding out the best places to visit. On the top of my list was a trip in the Banff gondola, which would take me to the top of the world, apparently.

The leaflets and the locals weren't wrong. It was, perhaps, the most beautiful scenery I had ever had the pleasure of witnessing. The Rockies were spectacular, and to see them from a glass box so high up was simply awe-inspiring.

At the top, I walked for a little while, having a coffee in the nearby Starbucks before heading back down to town so I could chill out for an hour before dinner.

oOo

I STOOD LEANING at the entrance to the wooden cabin, a hot cup of coffee in my hands as I surveyed my home for the next couple of days. It was staggering. Apparently, there was a waterfall located not far away, and I planned to hike down to find it after breakfast. I could take my time. After all, it was just me. I smiled, remembering the past few days; I'd seen a lot of Banff and the surrounding areas, taking a dip in the hot springs being one of my favourite few hours, whiling away the time as if I had so much of it – which I did! I had nothing to go back to. I could do whatever I wanted, whenever I wanted to do it, and that alone made me smile.

Waving to the people who were staying in the cabin next door, I pushed the door to and went to put my coffee cup in the sink before getting ready.

Ten minutes later, I had my sturdy shoes on, the ones I'd bought a couple of days into my trip for all the walking I intended to do, and was ready to go. With a map in my little backpack, just in case, I followed the signs for the waterfall, walking among the most enormous trees, down along some steep rocks before I found some steps to follow. I heard the water before I finally came upon it, and when I did, it took my breath away. It wasn't particularly huge or anything, but it was the colour of the water that struck me. It was the most beautiful shade of light blue. Magical. Truly magical.

All of a sudden, my imagination began to run wild, and I grinned, looking around me. I took a few photos and then took the bag off my back, searching for the notebook and pen I'd brought with me. I found a spot to sit down and proceeded to make notes of everything in my head. Mermaids, monsters, creatures of the dark. They all invaded my space for about an hour until I'd written as much as I could possibly write in that little book.

Ecstatic, I knew I had the bones for a brand new series, and I couldn't wait to see more of this beautiful country. This was going to be the beginning of something seriously exciting.

The next day I drove into Jasper. It made me chuckle because I couldn't help but think of the character from Twilight. Sad really; but hey, that's me. I chuckled again as I parked the car and went off to have a wander. I found some really cool shops, full of beautiful local crafts and Canadian-made jewellery. I bought a few postcards and watched people go by as I sat with a hot chocolate and a slice of cake, before heading back to the car. I spent the rest of the day hiking through various beauty spots in the vicinity. Even though I was alone, not once did I feel lonely. It was perhaps the best, yet saddest, time of my life.

oOo

THE NEXT FEW days were spent driving across Alberta, stopping overnight a couple of times, before heading through British Columbia and staying in the beautiful holiday resort of Whistler, where I spent two nights. I remembered watching some of the winter Olympics there on TV a while back and thought how lovely it looked. I was right, of course. The town had a real buzz to it. There was so much to do – hiking, biking, skiing (although that wasn't possible at that time of year), shopping, eating and so on. It was full of young and old, all enjoying the beautiful blue skies and the crisp air.

Leaving it behind, I headed across to Vancouver Island, where I eventually found the little town of Tofino. I think I might have left a little bit of my heart there, actually. Famous for its vast white sandy beaches, much of them covered in the most enormous pieces of driftwood, it was easy to understand why it was so popular with surfers. In fact the town seemed to be so full of them, it was hard to spot anyone else!

My house for a few nights was right on the beach. It was stunning. On two levels, the open plan kitchen, dining room and lounge were on the ground floor, but my favourite part was upstairs. A grand bedroom with a couple of steps upwards led to a large sunken bath with a view out to the beach. It was absolute heaven. My first night was spent drinking wine in the tub. It was the first time my mind drifted...

The feeling of dancing in the rain, being entirely at ease with each other, doing whatever the mood drove us to. Dancing in the rain. I sighed, took a long swig of the wine, letting it slowly slide down my throat, my muscles relaxed as it hit the spot, and I closed my eyes again.

Flashes of his hands, the way they cupped my bum as he pulled me towards him in the pool. His face as he dropped his head back with laughter, his body drenched in rain as he danced to Singin' in the Rain, his fingers deftly wrapping my foot in a bandage as we

166

sat on the chaise-longue, his tongue on my skin, my inner thighs, his romantic proposal in the storm, his kiss...

I woke with a start, dropping the wine into the bath.

'Shit,' I said as I wobbled, grabbing the now empty glass and placing it on the side of the bath. It was only then that I realised I'd been crying.

Looking out of the window and wiping my eyes, I noticed it was raining, just a gentle pitter-patter against the window. Turning the hot tap back on, I felt the warmth drift up from my feet, knees, thighs, between my legs and I sighed. It felt good, that warmth. I wanted more. I wanted to feel like a woman again; like a sexual woman. I groaned at the thought and placed my fingers between my legs, slowly sliding them up and down, making my mouth open as I imagined being kissed again. I slid further down the bath and arched my back, caressing my breasts, before sliding my finger firmly inside myself, careful to let my palm rub against my clitoris. Increasing both pressure and speed, I felt my body respond and soon, I let out a little groan as I came. Guilt flooded me.

Why feel guilty for pleasuring yourself? said the devil. You're your own woman. You're single. It's your body and if it feels good, then great! Don't feel guilty, she said, and I smiled. I was beginning to think the devil and the angel were one and the same.

Sitting in the water, I slumped forward and looked down at my watch. Twenty past eight. My stomach grumbled as if on cue. Unplugging the bath, I sat for a moment, letting the water flood down the hole, before I stood up and grabbed a towel. I dried myself off and put on the fluffy white dressing gown provided by the owners of the rental property, then padded down the stairs into the kitchen.

Half an hour later, I sat at the dining table with a bowl of tomato pasta and another glass of white wine in front of me. I was just about to tuck in when I heard a noise outside.

I froze waiting. I'd read all about bears living in Canada, and I certainly didn't want to encounter one. When nothing else happened, I twirled the spaghetti around the fork and began to eat dinner. Just two minutes later, there was a knock on the door.

Strange.

Pulling the gown tight against my body, I unlocked and opened the door.

'Adam,' I gasped, leaning against the frame for support.

'Hi, Eve,' he replied, looking utterly exhausted and drenched through.

'What are you doing here? How did you know where to come? What...' but before I continued, I sighed. 'Mum?'

He nodded. 'Can I come in?'

I held the door open and stepped aside in absolute shock. He took off his coat, not really knowing what to do with it, sopping wet as it was. Because I did nothing, he opened the front door again and just hung it on the door handle before shutting it.

He shivered.

'Oh God, you're wet through,' I said, pulling myself together. 'I'll get you a towel.' I left him standing in the kitchen and slowly walked up the stairs to the bedroom.

Once inside I shut the door and sat on the bed, taking deep breaths. I actually pinched myself; I couldn't quite believe he had travelled halfway across the world to find me. But why now? If I was what he truly wanted, why hadn't he reached out to me before? I was pulled from feeling angry to a deep sense of relief and happiness. But I let the anger win over, and I stood up, grabbing a towel before rushing back downstairs.

'Adam, what are you doing here?' I demanded, passing it to him.

He took it, looking so lost. 'I...I...came to find you, Eve. I needed to see you...'

'You needed to see me? Why? Why come all this way? You shouldn't be here, Adam. You should have stayed away.'

'But, but...'

'But what, Adam?'

'I love you,' he said quietly.

'No, you don't. It's clear to me now. You never loved me, not really.'

'You're wrong, Eve.'

I shook my head and turned away, grabbing my wine from the dining table and taking a swig.

'Eve, I do love you. More than you could ever understand.'

'No, you loved Lisa, and now that she's gone, you don't want to be alone.'

Adam let the towel hang around his neck as he stepped forward and took my hand in his. 'No, you don't really believe that, do you? Please, Eve. I'm sorry, truly sorry for causing you so much pain. I never meant to, you know?'

I turned to face him, letting him pull me closer to him. 'I know, Adam. I know you didn't do this on purpose. But we weren't meant to be. You shouldn't have come here.'

'No?' he asked.

I shook my head and pulled my hand away.

'Don't you love me?' he whispered, and my breath stuck in my throat. 'I know you love me, Eve. Please don't push me away now. Tell me the truth... don't you love me?'

I sobbed and stepped away.

'Eve, please,' he said, tears falling down his cheeks. 'I love you so much, and I want to make it up to you for the rest of my life.'

'Adam, no. I can't take any more of this.'

'Say it, say you don't love me anymore.'

I opened my mouth to say it, but the words wouldn't come. How could I lie?

'Oh, Adam,' I cried, falling into his arms. 'I do love you, but I can't bear all this pain.'

'I'll never hurt you again, Eve. I promise.'

I looked up into his eyes and saw such love there. I wanted him. I'd always wanted him. But he hadn't been ready. Was he ready now?

As I sat on his lap on the sofa, he pulled me towards him, and our lips finally met in a tantalisingly erotic kiss that had every nerve ending through my body tingling with desire.

'Evie... I want you so bad,' he whispered into my ear. 'I've missed you so much. I was devastated when you left.'

Standing up, I took his hand and led him slowly upstairs to the bedroom, where I pushed him back onto the bed. For a minute, I left him there so I could go and put the plug back into the bath and started rerunning it. For some reason, I really wanted to have a bath with him. Then I returned to him and slowly removed his clothes. He just sat there, watching me as each shoe and sock was dropped to the floor. I unbuckled his belt and slowly pulled it through the loops, throwing it behind me. Next was his sweater; he held his arms up so I could slide it off. I took a few moments to unbutton his shirt, then I pulled it open, sliding my hands over his torso before sliding them down his jeans as he shrugged out of the shirt. I undid the top button teasingly slowly before the next. Then I pulled him to his feet so I could pull them down past his thighs. He lifted each leg, allowing me to remove them and fling them across the room. He stood in nothing but his boxer shorts, his erection straining against the fabric.

I pulled at the elastic, letting it snap back against his skin with a half-smile.

His face was flushed with desire as I slowly put my hands down the back of his shorts and cupped his rock hard buttocks, pulling him towards me. He groaned as his hardness pressed against my skin.

Then I pushed him away and ran up the few steps so I could turn the tap off, before returning to remove his final piece of clothing. But before I did, I let my dressing gown drop to the floor.

Adam stared at me, admiring my nudity, as I crouched down, so my face was level with his crotch, then I used my fingers to gently pull down the shorts until they were on the floor. His hardness rested against my neck, and I nuzzled it for a second before I slowly stood up, rubbing my entire body against him deliciously.

I took his hand and led him up the stairs, where we both climbed into the tub. He lay back, and I straddled him, grinding against him, leaning forward to breathe in what I'd been missing for so long. His scent filled me.

'I've wanted this for so long, Adam,' I whispered. 'But I thought I'd lost you for good.'

'Me too,' he said, 'I'm sorry I hurt you. I'm sorry for all the pain I caused you. But I'm here now, and I'm not going anywhere. I love you, Eve,' he whispered into my ear, while his hands searched every part of my body, probing, stroking, fingering. His lips sucked wherever they could reach above the hot water. My body pulsed with desire as I eventually lifted myself up and lowered myself so that he filled me. A loud groan erupted from both of our lips as his tongue investigated my mouth, and he sucked my tongue erotically. I lifted and lowered myself slowly as he used his fingers to gently massage my clitoris and bottom at the same time, his fingers sliding up and down, rubbing from side to side. I pulled away, lifting myself off him before turning to face the other way, while his fingers continued to probe every part of me.

It was like nothing before, not even our first time in London. This was different.

'Let's get out,' he suggested from behind me.

I nodded, and we climbed out. Before we could get down the steps though, he was fucking me from behind, and I groaned before pulling away from him, so we could at least make it down to the carpet.

I made him lie on the soft floor and leaned over him, taking him in my mouth, gently playing with him using only my tongue. He turned me around so he could easily use his own probing tongue to gently caress me. I had to stop to get my breath back, groaning louder and louder by the second. Not wanting to come just yet, and wanting him back inside me, I turned back around and straddled him, fucking him harder and harder until the inevitable happened and we both came together in a blissful state of happiness.

CHAPTER 30

I squealed at the sight of a Beluga whale gliding across the massive pool behind the glass. It was the most astounding creature I'd ever seen, the way it moved through the water was mesmerising. I just stood, staring at it for a few minutes. The click of a camera distracted me, and I turned to see Adam taking another photo of me with the whale at my side. I grinned.

'Isn't it just the most beautiful sight you've ever seen?' I asked.

He looked at me and nodded. 'She certainly is,' he teased, ruffling my hair with his hands. 'I do love your hair like this, you know?'

'I know. You keep telling me.'

'You just look so cute,' he said as he grabbed my hand. 'Come on, there's tonnes more to see.'

He pulled me through Vancouver Aquarium until we got to the sloths, the animal he'd been going on about since we'd arrived. They were so fascinating to watch, almost appearing unreal, like teddy bears.

'They don't look real,' I said as we looked up to see them hanging from the branches of the trees above us.

'They're definitely real,' he replied. 'Look at that one, it's eating something,' he pointed.

'Speaking of eating, I'm starving. Shall we go and find a cafe?' I suggested. When I saw his face, I added, 'We can always come back to the sloths, babe.'

Smiling, Adam nodded. 'I think I saw one this way.'

With coffee and cake on the table in front of us, we sat looking at each other, smiling.

'What?' I asked. 'What are you smiling at?'

'I'll tell you what I'm smiling about if you tell me what you're smiling about,' he teased.

'Okay, after three. One, two, three... YOU!' we both said a little louder than we should have done. People in the cafe looked at us with raised eyebrows, and the two of us fell about laughing before we quietened down a bit.

'So, how's the writing going? I'm sorry I haven't asked about it until now.'

'It's amazing. I spent the first few days scribbling like a mad woman. I've been so inspired by this place, Adam. It's so beautiful. And now that you're here, everything is perfect. I've finally got my mojo back.'

He grinned and squeezed my hand, 'I'm glad, babe. What have you been writing? Something new and exciting?'

I smiled shyly. 'It's going to be a new series for teenagers. A supernatural series with mermaids, monsters, vampires and stuff.'

'Really?" he asked, 'that sounds like something Amy would like. She loves all that stuff.'

'Maybe she could be the first person to read it for me when it's finished?'

'Eve, she would be honoured. I just know it.'

'Maybe Clare would like to read it too,' I teased.

He raised one eyebrow and then laughed. 'I'll ask her too, don't worry.'

'What about you? How's work been, by the way? I can't believe we're only just getting round to talking about all this stuff.'

'We've kind of had a lot going on,' he said sadly, leaning forward to kiss the side of my face.

'Yes, we certainly have,' I replied, turning my head so that my lips caught his. The sound of someone clearing their throat made us both move away, embarrassed. We didn't look up to see who didn't approve of our embrace.

'Erm, Eden Grove, yes,' Adam said, 'It's going well. The same as before, really. But I'm considering selling it.'

'Oh? Just one of the garden centres? Like before?'

'Before?' he asked.

'Yes, the first time we met in London, you said you were there to sell a garden centre.'

Adam smiled. 'You've got a good memory. Yes, that was one that wasn't doing so well, so I decided to get rid of it. But this time, I'm thinking of selling the entire business.'

'Why?' I asked, sipping the hot coffee.

'I'd like a little more time to devote to me... and you.'

'Adam,' I breathed. 'You're going to sell your business for me?'

'That's pretty much it, yes. After what happened with Lisa,' he paused for a second to take a breath, 'it made me realise that life is so precious and sometimes so short. I don't want to be apart from you again, Eve.'

'Gosh, I don't know what to say.'

'Eve, you are my everything. I don't want to be pulled away to the other side of the country on business anymore. I never want to be too far from your side. I've made some mistakes over the past few months, and like I said before, I need to make things up to you. I don't want to leave your side ever again.'

My stomach did little somersaults, and I grinned, resting my head on his shoulder. 'I don't want you to be, either.'

'Then that's settled. I'll email my lawyer later today. Have you finished?' he asked.

I nodded.

'Then let's go and celebrate with the sloths,' he laughed, pulling me up from my seat and kissing me passionately for all the patrons of the cafe to see.

As we were walking out, I turned to see an elderly couple looking very embarrassed, a group of teenagers were grinning and nudging each other, and the woman behind the till nodded at us with a smile.

oOo

IT WAS our last day in Canada, and if I'd been alone, I would have been saddened by that fact. But with Adam by my side, it didn't matter where in the world I was. Walking through the shopping district, I stopped to fantasise outside a designer boutique, looking at the Prada handbags and Louboutin shoes.

'Why don't you go in?' Adam asked.

'Nah, no point. I couldn't spend that kind of money on something like that.'

'Why not? You're buying quality.'

'No, you're buying the name.'

'Yes, I suppose that too. But it's an investment. You can always sell designer stuff later when you've had enough of it. Come on, let's have a look,' he insisted.

I relented and gingerly walked in, feeling decidedly out of place as the posh sales assistants looked us up and down the second we stepped over the threshold.

'This is nice,' Adam said, walking to a brown leather handbag.

'Adam, it's over a thousand dollars,' I said rigidly.

He looked at me and laughed, putting the bag back on the shelf. 'What about these? They're rather sexy, aren't they?' he said, picking up a pair of sky-high black patent heels with their trademark red sole.

'Holy shit,' I said, a little louder. 'Look at the price. Let's get out of here. I feel like everyone's looking at us.'

'Nobody's looking at us. You're imagining it,' he reassured me, as I looked around and realised he was absolutely right.

'Why not just try them on?' he suggested.

'No, I'm fine thanks,' I said, standing so close to him that he could barely breathe.

'Chill, Eve. Now sit down. What's your size? UK six, right?' I nodded, doing precisely as I was told.

He walked over to the sales assistant and smiled; they talked for a while, and she grinned at him before disappearing, returning moments later with the right size.

I took off my boot and sock as she removed the beautifully-made shoe from its box and then from within the cloth bag and placed it on my foot. I felt like Cinderella as it slipped on just like it had been made only for me.

'And the other one,' Adam said.

I removed my other boot and sock, and she carefully placed it on, and I stood up. They were a little higher than any shoes I'd ever had, and I struggled to gain my balance, but after a couple of moments, I looked at Adam and grinned. He watched as I walked from one end of the shop to the other.

'Wow,' he muttered. 'They look beautiful on you.'

'Yes, they do.'

'Are they comfortable?' he asked.

'Surprisingly so, considering their height,' I replied before sitting back down and removing them, reluctantly handing them back to the young woman.

'Well, I can now say that I've worn a pair of Louboutins.' I smiled as she put them back into the box, and I put my socks and boots back on. In the meantime, Adam wandered off to browse the designer wares for gentlemen.

Once I was ready, I stood up and looked around for him. After a couple of minutes or so, he appeared and smiled at me.

'See anything you like?'

'Nah, nothing really.'

'Let's go then.'

He took my hand, and we walked out of the shop, the saleswoman smiling and saying goodbye as we left.

'I can't imagine spending that amount of money on a pair of shoes, even if I was a millionaire,' I said as we wandered back down the street.

'I'm sure you would, babe.'

But I shook my head. 'It just seems like an obscene amount of money for a pair of shoes.'

'They were comfortable though, right?' he asked

I nodded and smiled. 'Very.'

'And I bet they made you feel like a million dollars too, right?'

I thought about it for a second and relented. 'Yes, I suppose they did.'

'Now imagine wearing them with a nice dress...'

'Oh yes, that would be nice.'

Adam laughed and squeezed my hand. 'Exactly my point.'

'Point taken.'

I was absolutely exhausted after the journey home and was so happy to walk through the door and just be alone, the two of us.

Neither one of us could barely lift our bags, so we just went straight to bed and slept for fifteen hours straight, waking up at two in the afternoon, completely famished.

I gently blew into Adam's ear until he woke up. Opening his eyes, he smiled.

'Afternoon, sleepyhead,' I whispered.

Smiling, he grabbed me and pulled me back down under the covers. I yelped and tried to get away, but he held on tight until I stopped playing and let him kiss me tenderly.

'Wow,' I whispered. 'Now that was a kiss.'

Adam simply smiled before he sat up. I jumped out of bed, and he smacked my bum as I walked past him, then I leaned over to him and grabbed him.

'Come on, get out of bed.'

He followed me and led me to the kitchen.

I raised one eyebrow. 'I guess we probably need to go food shopping; is there anything to eat in the meantime?' I asked, opening the massive fridge and stopping dead still to find it was fully stocked.

'How the hell?'

'Jack came down yesterday morning and sorted it out for us.'

'Jack, I love you.' I sighed, pulling out eggs, bacon, sausages, mushrooms and tomatoes.

'Full English? Sounds perfect,' Adam smiled. 'Why don't you let me do it? You could make some coffee?' he suggested.

Eventually, we had devoured a man-sized full English breakfast and several cups of coffee. Both of us sat back and sighed happily.

'That's better,' he said, rubbing his tummy.

'Shower now?' I said.

'I have a better idea,' he grinned.

'On such a full stomach?'

'Actually, I was thinking of a nice warm bath. What were you thinking?' he teased.

'Swimming pool,' I grinned.

'Let's save that for when our breakfast has gone down.'

I felt a tingle of anticipation between my legs just thinking about it.

'Just make sure that Jack has no plans to stop by,' I joked, as I cleared everything from the table and started to stack the dishwasher.

'Don't worry, we're quite safe. He's visiting Amy in Bournemouth this weekend,' he said, stopping me from cleaning, instead pulling me towards him so he could plant a deep kiss on my lips. I sighed with happiness.

CHAPTER 32

I'd missed Lisa's funeral, but I was happy to be there for her memorial service.

People of all ages dressed in all colours mingled throughout the manor. I smiled at the sight of everyone. It had been one of Lisa's last requests; she didn't want people to wear black at her memorial service. She wanted them to wear their favourite colour. She also didn't want anything morbid playing either, only her favourite songs. It was such a lovely idea, and it really made people talk to each other about what colours, music, and things were favoured to each of them, including the favourite things they remembered about this remarkable and loving young woman. Lisa Oakwood had only been forty-five years old.

I watched from the side of the room as Amy sat on Lisa's favourite armchair with her beautiful little baby in her arms. Clare sat on the floor beside them, gazing at them with pure love. Jack walked over to them and handed them both a glass of wine. Clare took it, but Amy shook her head.

'I can't drink while she's breastfeeding, bro,' she scolded.

'Oh,' he said, a little embarrassed. 'I'll get you some juice.' He disappeared, returning seconds later with a glass of apple juice.

'Thanks.' She smiled up at him.

There were lots of people I'd never met, and everyone had come over to me and offered their condolences. All mentioned that Lisa had told them about me, and they were all grateful that she had such a dear friend at the end of her life. I was touched, to say the least.

'Eve?' said Jack from behind me. I turned nervously as he handed me a glass of sherry. 'Good to see you.'

'Thanks, Jack. How are you holding up?' I asked.

He shrugged. 'It's hard.'

'It is. But it must be even harder for you.'

He looked at me questioningly.

'Boys are often a little closer to their mothers. She loved you so much, Jack. She told me all about you as a little boy. She said you were such a rascal, but you were also such a mummy's boy.'

Jack smiled and nodded. 'Yes, you can say that again. She used to spoil me. She never stopped, really.'

'I'm so sorry, Jack.'

His lips pursed as he tried not to well up again. 'I miss her.'

'Me too.'

'I still can't believe she's gone.'

'I know.'

He looked at me in a strange way before walking away, disappearing into the crowd.

'Hey,' said Clare, who was stretching her legs and holding the tiny little bundle in her arms. 'How was your trip?'

I looked at her, a little embarrassed. 'Hey, Clare. It was good. Look, I'm sorry I just left like that.'

'Don't worry, we all understood why you had to go.'

I smiled. 'How are you enjoying motherhood?'

'It's so amazing, Eve. I've never felt anything like this before. It's a bit of a struggle with Amy's emotions at the moment, though. It's been a tough few weeks, let's just put it that way.'

'It'll get easier. She just needs a little time to come to terms with everything.'

Clare nodded. 'You know we both feel that a little bit of Lisa's soul was born again with the baby?'

I smiled. 'I would agree with that. The way it happened? It was like it was meant to be. Oh yes, Lisa is definitely still here,' I said, looking down at the most beautiful little child.

'Would you like to hold her?' asked Amy, who was walking towards us.

'Really?' I asked, shocked. I'd never actually held such a tiny little baby before. Not one as young as this, anyway.

'Of course,' she replied as Clare handed her to me.

'We're actually calling her Junior at the moment,' Amy added. 'It's a bit hard to call her Lisa right now,' she said, brushing the tears from her eyes.

'Hello, Junior,' I whispered. The second I said her name, she opened her eyes wide and looked up at me, and my heart melted.

'Oh,' I said, breathing deeply.

'What's wrong?' Clare asked.

'Nothing's wrong. She's absolutely perfect,' I smiled.

'Your aura is going through the roof right now,' Clare whispered into my ear, and I grinned.

'I can imagine.'

CHAPTER 33

he following morning, after I'd had a cup of coffee and some toast, I headed upstairs to the room I'd made into my office. It hadn't been decorated like my previous one in my old home, but I had plans.

I closed the door quietly and sat down at the little desk. It was the first time I'd been in there since Lisa had died. Opening the top drawer, I was surprised to find an envelope with my name on it.

Frowning, I opened it and recognised Lisa's handwriting, albeit a little more scrawled than usual. She must have written this near the end.

EVIE, my dearest friend.

I know we only had a short time together as friends, but it became clear to me from the start that you were my soul mate pal, if you know what I mean? lol

I just wanted you to know a few things that you might not be aware of. Firstly, I am so happy that you and Adam are together. I know that he and I have had a strange relationship over the years, and when you came on the scene, it might have confused you a little. He and I always loved each other deeply. At certain points, we were in love. Possibly even recently, but he is meant for you.

You and he complement each other in ways that he and I never did.

I realise my passing is going to be exceedingly hard on him, and I'm sure he will feel alone and lost. I was always the one he turned to, so I need you to become that person, Eve. I need you to not only be his lover (!) but to be his best friend. He needs you more than you know. Just like I needed you more than you realised.

Eve, you don't realise what a remarkable woman you are. I just wanted you to know that. My kids are very fond of you too. I know shortly after my diagnosis, they struggled with the idea of you but seeing you care for me and seeing you love their father has changed that. You were never a mother, Evie, but you will make a damn good stepmother and a wonderful grandma. Lucky you! That is my only regret that I will never get to meet my grandchild.

Thank you for being you, Eve. And thank you for loving us... when you really didn't have to.

With much love

Your soul mate pal, Lisa

xxx

TEARS FLOODED MY EYES, and I sobbed and sobbed for what felt like hours. If I'd found this letter before I'd disappeared to Canada, would I have still gone? I couldn't stop crying. Until that is, the sight of the sunlight catching the little crystal near the window caused beams of colourful light to fill the room. I felt like Lisa was there with me, warming me and encouraging me to be the real me again. Something I needed to do for myself and for Adam.

I smiled. 'Thanks Lisa,' I whispered and stood up, leaving the room.

Adam was nowhere to be seen. I looked in every room in the house before a thought occurred to me and I headed outside, through to the swimming pool.

Adam was sitting with his feet in the water. He looked up, surprised when I approached him.

'Hey,' I said.

'Hey.'

'How are you feeling?' I asked as I rolled up my jeans and sat beside him, letting my feet dangle in the warm water.

'Okay, I guess,' he said with a sad smile.

'I miss her too.'

He frowned and nodded. 'I'm so glad you're here.'

'I'm glad I'm here too.' I smiled.

'It's strange that it's all over.'

'You mean the memorial service?' I asked him.

He nodded.

'Lisa will always be here with us, Adam. We won't ever forget her. But it's you and me now, babe.'

'You and me.' He smiled. 'I love you so much, Eve. Come on, let me prove it to you.' A wicked grin spread across his face as he started removing his clothes.

'You coming in?' he asked me.

I didn't need asking twice.

CHAPTER 34

*W*andering through my favourite city of Bath, hand in hand, Adam pulled me towards the jeweller's he'd previously mentioned.

'This is the one,' he said, dragging me inside.

'Adam, we can't start looking yet. It's not right.'

'Why not?'

'Because we need to wait for my divorce to be finalised.'

'You spoke to your lawyer yesterday, right?'

I nodded.

'And she said it should be a matter of weeks?'

I nodded again.

'Well, there you go. Then we can get married.'

'But I won't feel right about buying our wedding rings until then.'

'Okay, but there's no harm in looking, is there?'

Shrugging, I let him pull me to the counter while he asked the assistant to show us their selection of wedding rings. They were pulled out in a large case as we perused each and every one.

'This one's beautiful,' Adam said, pulling out a ring that was a little too masculine for me.

'I thought you wanted matching rings?' I asked, disappointed.

'Yes, you don't like this?'

'It's huge. I've only got skinny fingers, babe.'

Adam laughed and handed it back to the assistant.

'How about this one?' I pointed to one which would look lovely on both of us.

'It's a little boring, don't you think?'

'Not really.'

'How about this?' he said, lifting an exquisite ring that had little diamonds running all along it.

'Oh yes, that's stunning,' I sighed. 'I bet it's ridiculously expensive, though.'

'The price isn't an issue, so don't worry about it. Try it on,' he said, taking it out of the assistant's hand and placing it carefully on my finger.

'Wow,' I sighed. 'It really is something special, isn't it?'

Adam nodded, 'I think we've found our wedding rings.'

'But we have to wait. Okay?'

'Sure. Thank you,' he said to the girl behind the counter. 'We'll be back in a few weeks to order them.'

She smiled and nodded. 'Great. See you then. Enjoy your engagement.'

'Our engagement.' I laughed when we walked out of the shop. I hadn't quite thought of us as being engaged. It sounded a little weird, especially after me running away and the fact that I was still officially married to Matt. Not for long, though, and the thought made me smile.

'So we should start talking about the wedding,' Adam said, as he took my hand in his and we started walking down the crowded street in the centre of the city.

'Yes, I suppose we should.' I grinned. 'But not on an empty tummy.'

Adam rubbed my stomach and laughed, 'No. We can't do anything on an empty belly. What do you fancy? Cornish Pasty?'

'Mmmm I haven't had a Cornish Pasty for ages.'

'There's the perfect place just down here,' he said, pulling me down to the corner of the street where the delicious aroma of freshly baked pasties filled the air. 'Smells divine, doesn't it?'

I nodded as we walked in and ordered two to take away. We

went back outside, snuggled next to each other on a street bench and tucked in. The meat and potato pasties really were delicious.

Just as we were finishing up, Adam put his hand on my knee and kissed me lightly on the lips. 'Now, I'm not taking no for an answer.'

'No to what?' I asked curiously.

'There's something I want you to do for me.'

'Erm, okay?'

He stood up first and pulled me to my feet. Smiling, we walked for ten minutes until we stopped outside a bridal shop.

'What are we doing here?' I asked.

'I'd like to see you try on some wedding dresses.' He grinned.

'Really? But it's supposed to be bad luck for the groom to see his bride in her dress before the big day?'

'Yes, but there's no harm in trying them on, is there?' he encouraged.

'I don't suppose so,' I relented. 'I've never tried wedding dresses on before.'

'But what about your wedding to Matt?' he asked.

'It was borrowed from my cousin because we couldn't afford to buy one at the time.'

'Oh, that's sad. You deserve to have the full bridal experience. Let's have some fun today. And then perhaps you could come back with Amy and Clare? I'm sure they'd love to be involved with the wedding plans.'

'Really? You think they would?'

'Actually, I know they would. I asked them, and they both squealed like little girls,' he laughed.

'In that case, let's do it. I can get an idea today of the kind of style I'd like to wear when I marry the man of my dreams.'

Adam squeezed my bum as we pushed open the door to the beautifully decorated wedding boutique. It was fitted all in white, pale pink and grey.

'Good afternoon,' said a pretty little woman dressed in a grey pinstripe suit. 'Do you have an appointment?'

'Oh, sorry, no. We can come back another day,' I said.

She smiled. 'No need. We actually had a cancellation earlier so feel free to come through. I'm Louise, by the way. I'll be your stylist today.'

'Thank you very much, Louise,' Adam said, as we followed her through to another much larger room, where a couple of wedding dresses were placed on mannequins in both corners.

We could hear laughter in an adjacent room but thought nothing of it.

'Now tell me, what sort of look are you going for?' asked Louise.

I looked across at Adam. I'd not given it a single thought. I hadn't got a clue. He looked at me, equally lost.

Louise laughed, 'Don't worry. I get a lot of brides coming in that have no idea what they're looking for. When and where are you getting married? Perhaps that will help?

Again, we both looked at each other and laughed nervously.

'Right,' Louise said, clapping her hands together. 'Formal event?'

Adam and I both shook our heads.

'Summer? Winter? Spring?'

I twisted my lips to one side as I thought about it.

'Spring?' we both said at once.

Louise chuckled. 'Looks like we're actually planning your wedding right now.'

'You've no idea,' I said.

'Do you like satin, silk, taffeta, lace?'

'Lace, I love lace.' I smiled.

'White, ivory, cream, champagne, pink, purple, black?' she giggled.

'Actually, now that you mention it,' I said. 'I do like pale colours with a touch of black.'

Adam raised his eyebrows and nodded. 'Hmm, I quite like the sound of that.'

Louise nodded her head. 'I think I have a couple of options that might just be perfect on you. Why don't you come through, erm, sorry, I didn't get your names?'

'Eve,' I said.

'I'm Adam,' he said.

Louise looked at me, then at Adam with a frown.

'We're actually serious. Adam and Eve, that's us. No joke.'

'Goodness me,' chuckled Louise. 'Obviously destined to be together.'

Fifteen minutes later, I stood in front of a long mirror wearing the most beautiful, figure-hugging lace gown in ivory. Around the waist was a black sash and a hint of black lace at the cap sleeve.

Adam wolf-whistled as I walked out for him to see.

'My, my,' he said. 'That's beautiful. You look breath-taking, Eve,' he said deliciously.

'Why thank you,' I said, turning back to the other mirror. 'It's definitely along the right lines, but there's a couple of things I'm not keen on, so perhaps I could try the next one?'

Louise nodded. 'Absolutely.'

Just as we were turning to go back through to the changing room, the laughter in the next room intensified and before I had the time to say a word, a couple walked out, and I stood face to face with Matt and Charlie.

'Eve?' Matt stuttered. 'Wow, you look incredible.'

'Erm, hello, Matt, Charlie. How are you both?'

'Good, thank you. It's lovely to see you, darlin'. How have you been?' Charlie asked a little nervously as I played with my engagement ring.

'Good, thanks, very good.'

'I see congratulations are in order,' she said. 'When's the big day?'

'We're... erm, not sure yet. Obviously, we're waiting for the divorce to come through. You're getting married too, huh?' I asked nervously.

'Everything alright back here?' said Adam as he walked into the hallway and saw who I was talking to.

'Oh, Charlie. Matt.' He nodded, looking at me with wide eyes.

'You're marrying Adam?' Charlie shrieked. 'Oh my God, I can't believe it. That's... that's... amazing!'

'Erm, yes it is, isn't it?' Adam replied with a grin as he approached me and put his arm protectively on my lower back.

'Congratulations,' Matt muttered.

'What are the chances, eh?' Charlie said. 'And of us meeting in a wedding shop, of all places. You must come to our wedding. It's obviously a sign.' She hugged me. 'I'm so glad things have worked out for you both. I must confess, I'm a little surprised, Adam. I thought you'd go back to Lisa,' she winked.

'Actually, Lisa died.'

Charlie's eyes widened, and the smile dropped from her face. 'Oh, Jesus, Adam. I'm so sorry, darlin'. What happened? When? Are the kids alright?' she asked with obvious concern.

'Cancer. Not long ago. It happened pretty quickly,' Adam answered, choking up a little.

'We're all struggling with it, to be honest,' I continued. 'But at least we all had time to say goodbye. Amy's little girl was born on the very same day. Can you believe that?'

'Really?' Charlie said, wiping her eyes. 'That's incredible.'

Adam nodded.

'But what about your little girl?' I asked quietly. 'Where is she?'

'My sister's looking after her today.' Charlie smiled, clearly embarrassed.

Changing the subject, Matt spoke. 'I'm sorry for your loss, Adam,' he said quietly, clearly uncomfortable.

'Thanks,' Adam replied, equally uncomfortable.

'Have you set a date yet?' I asked them both.

Matt smiled. 'Yes. The 1st of January. We figured the divorce would be through by then.'

'I certainly hope so, that's months away.' Adam smiled as he tried to finally let go of the past.

'Would you like to come?' Matt asked, looking at us both hopefully.

'Are you sure that's a good idea?' I replied.

'Of course it is. We were thinking of asking you, but weren't sure if it would be a bit too weird,' he said, looking at me before turning his head to Adam hopefully.

'If you'd really like us to come, then we'd be delighted to. Right, Adam?'

Adam slowly grinned and nodded. 'Actually, that would be

wonderful. We always used to get on so well, so maybe it's time that we forgive and forget. Why shouldn't we try again?'

Matt visibly relaxed and breathed out a deep sigh. 'I was worried you were going to punch me or something,' he smiled.

Adam and I both laughed.

'Water under the bridge, Matt. Water under the bridge.'

Charlie and Matt's wedding was as gaudy as her bedroom design, but it was perfect. It was so them. Adam and I both noticed people looking at us weirdly when we first arrived, but soon the guests started to loosen up and made a few jokes about swapping partners, but all was said in relatively good taste. We ended up having a blast. It was the first time we'd genuinely let our hair down (and mine was getting a little longer again) in a while, and it was both exciting and relaxing.

Charlie wore a long, princess-style dress, complete with pink tiara, while Matt's suit was a pale grey with a pink tie that matched the pink in her dress. They were a beautiful couple. Certainly well suited, both in looks and in character, and their first dance just proved how in love they were. They only had eyes for each other, and we knew it wouldn't be long until there were more babies between them.

The reception took place in a small 'castle', where large open fires cackled in several of the rooms to warm the place up. It was a freezing cold day outside, and the guests huddled together while all the photos were taken. Fortunately, Charlie had the foresight to bring an enormous white fake-fur coat to wear in-between pictures. She looked like a movie star, and Matt was treating her like one, carrying her across the snow for a unique photo in front of the forest at the back of the property. He nearly dropped her though, and most of the guests fell about laughing. It couldn't have been easy to carry a woman wearing such an over-sized dress.

Once we'd eaten as much food as we could possibly fit in, the lighting was changed to that of a disco scene, the music changed, and everybody began to dance the night away. It was a memorable wedding, one I wouldn't forget for years to come. Adam and I had danced for much of the night, smooching to the love songs and kicking it back to the rock 'n roll and pop stuff.

After a while, I left him on the dance floor, where he was having fun with a few grannies, and went for some fresh air. Taking a glass of Champagne with me, I headed for the nearby terrace and crept out, closing it behind me. A few guests were running about outside squealing, but otherwise, it was pretty quiet.

I leaned on the wall, took a long sip of my drink, and smiled. Hearing the terrace door open, I looked back, expecting to see Adam, but was surprised to see Matt appear.

'Hey.' He smiled.

'Hi. It's a lovely wedding, Matt.'

'Yeah, thanks. We're delighted you and Adam decided to come.'

'We are too. It was lovely of you to invite us.'

Matt smiled and took a swig of his lager. 'How have you been? I mean, really?' he asked, looking out across the magnificent gardens.

'It was rough for a little while, but then I started to find myself and now, well. I couldn't be happier.'

He nodded. 'Your mum and dad alright?'

'They're same as always,' I laughed. 'They're coming to our wedding in April. If you come, you can see for yourself.'

He pulled a funny face. 'Maybe we should decline,' he laughed.

Chuckling, I said, 'No. Mum's just always worried about me. She won't attack you or anything. You'll be quite safe. But maybe you should bring some pepper spray, just in case.'

Matt nodded seriously. 'Thanks for the advice, I might just do that.' He grinned. 'Seriously though, Eve. I'm sorry we hurt you. I'm glad you've managed to come through it better than you were before.'

'Thanks, Matt. I have Adam to thank for that.'

'You were seeing him before weren't you?' Matt suddenly asked. When I blushed, he nodded knowingly.

'I...I...'

'It's okay. I probably drove you to him, anyway.'

'No-one's to blame, Matt. These things happen. We had some good times together, though. I've never regretted being married to you.'

'I never regretted you, either. It just wasn't meant to last, that's all.'

'I couldn't agree more. I'm glad that we're all friends again.'

'Me too,' he said, swigging back the last of his lager. 'I'd better get back inside.'

I nodded. 'Yes, I'll come with you. Adam's probably wondering where I've got to.'

oOo

'WHAT A WONDERFUL DAY,' I sighed in the back of the taxi on the way home.

'It was, wasn't it? Those two are perfect together.'

'Just like you and me,' I said, placing my hand seductively on his thigh.

'Just like you and me,' he repeated in a whisper, as my hand slowly reached higher and higher up his thigh.

'Weddings always make me horny, I wonder why,' I breathed into his ear.

He coughed and looked nervously at the driver who was either pretending to ignore us or really had no idea how horny his passengers really were.

'Relax,' I said. 'Just relax,' I licked my lips and kissed his ear before licking it.

Immediately I felt his erection straining beneath his suit trousers. 'Oh man,' he groaned quietly. 'Stop, you need to stop.'

But I ignored his pleas and continued to lick seductively.

He tried hard to resist my advances, and I could tell he was so relieved when we arrived home. 'You can just drop us off at the bottom of the drive,' Adam almost squeaked.

I laughed and took out some money from my purse, handing it to the driver, who winked as we climbed out.

I smiled cheekily as it drove away.

'I'm so embarrassed,' Adam coughed.

'He winked at me, you know?'

'Oh God,' he said, as we opened the gate and walked through.

'Come on, you sex kitten. Let's continue this upstairs,' he said, draping his arm over my shoulder, purposefully brushing his hand over my breasts.

'I have a better idea,' I purred. He looked at me knowingly, and the moment we opened the front door, he started to take off my clothes, leaving a trail of them through the house and along the back until we reached the swimming pool, where a faint haze sat above the water from the heat.

'Mmm, it looks so inviting,' I whispered.

'I know what looks inviting, and I'm not talking about the pool,' he said, grabbing me and lifting my naked body up. I wrapped my legs around his torso as he walked us into the water. I relaxed backwards, keeping my legs around him as I rubbed myself up and down him.

'Mmmmm, this is so good,' I breathed, as he leaned forward and kissed my neck, licking it, tasting me.

'It certainly is,' he whispered as I unwrapped my legs and swam out to the centre of the pool where I waited for him to follow me.

'Come and get me, big boy,' I said, clearly the alcohol releasing any inhibitions I might usually have.

He pounced on me and stuck his tongue in my mouth erotically, while his fingers stroked all the way down my back beneath the water, lower and lower until I groaned with utter pleasure before he slid them over my bottom and underneath me, making me giggle and groan at the same time.

He pulled me towards the steps and laid me down on the top one before he began kissing me from head to foot, all the while his fingers sliding in and out of me, as my body undulated towards him. I turned on my side and put his erection in my mouth while he continued to finger me. I moved gently at first and then harder and harder until I couldn't hold back any longer. I sat up and made him sit on the step where I straddled him, lowering myself so that he was comfortably inside of me. Up and down, I slid, pushing myself against him. He bit my nipple tantalizingly, and I pushed harder and deeper until I came first. One, two, three orgasms. I laughed and turned us both around so I could lean my elbows on the top step, then I accepted him from behind. He thrust deeper and deeper, making me squeal until I finally felt him shudder and then relax on top of me.

We swam for a few minutes before finally calling it a night at three o'clock in the morning.

CHAPTER 36

The day before our wedding, Adam and I visited the graves of his parents, and then we drove to the location where Lisa's ashes had been scattered. It was a beautiful meadow with a forest behind it – she'd discovered it on one of her many country walks she'd taken before falling ill. It had become her favourite place in the world, and she'd made Adam promise to let her rest there 'for eternity'.

'I feel her here, you know,' he said, as we held on to each other's hands and walked through the sopping wet grass. I shivered and smiled nodding.

'Me too. She's all around us, I just know it.'

He squeezed my hand as we approached a huge tree trunk, where we stopped and sat down for a moment, just enjoying the quietness, the soft sound of the breeze blowing through all those trees beyond.

'Do you believe in soul mates, Eve?' asked Adam.

I thought for a moment and nodded. 'But I think soul mates can come in many guises. Like Lisa, for instance. She told me we were soul mate pals,' I chuckled.

He patted my thigh and smiled.

'And you,' I added. 'I really think we were meant to be together. If that makes us soul mates, then so be it.'

'I've known for a while now that we are,' he replied.

'You have? How?'

He shrugged. 'I don't know. I just know. Maybe we were together in a previous existence?'

'Like I was Queen Victoria and you were Prince Albert?'

'Exactly,' he laughed. 'Or you were Marilyn Monroe, and I was, erm... Kennedy?'

'Soul mates? But they just had a fling,' I giggled, pushing him gently.

'He was the only one I could think of. How about Henry the Eighth and Anne Boleyn?'

'Adam!'

'What?' he replied innocently.

'She was beheaded! At her husband's request.'

'Oh,' Adam started laughing even more. 'I guess I'm not very good at this.'

'Maybe we were just two beautiful butterflies in our previous life?' I offered.

'That's nice. I like that idea. Or cats, maybe. Cats have such an easy life.'

I hugged him tightly. 'Yes, something like that.'

'I feel quite strongly about it, you know?'

'What? About us being cats or butterflies together?'

He chuckled. 'That too, but no. About us being soul mates. Fate was trying so hard to get us together. Why would she do that, unless we were soul mates?'

'You think fate is a she?' I asked.

'Naturally.' He smiled, kissing the end of my nose. 'Your nose is freezing,' he said, standing up and pulling me towards him so I could bury my face in his shoulder. 'I'm the happiest man in the world right now,' he sighed. 'I'm marrying the woman of my dreams tomorrow.'

I smiled and squeezed. I felt the same way. I couldn't believe that my life had turned out the way it had. I'd found a man who I adored with my very soul, who loved me back with such intensity. Our passion was nothing I'd ever experienced, and I looked forward to spending the rest of my life in the arms of this man. Not only that, but we were living in the most magnificent home.

My inspiration had rocketed, and my books were starting to sell like the proverbial hotcakes. Add to that an instant family in Amy, Jack, Clare and little Lisa Junior. How could I possibly be any happier?

Oh, yes... a wedding.

CHAPTER 37

*E*yes opening wide, I grinned and looked over at the bedside clock. Almost exactly seven o'clock. I rolled over; it had been such a strange night sleeping in an empty bed, but Adam was a little bit of a traditionalist and had wanted to spend the night apart.

I jumped up, put on my dressing gown and headed downstairs. I could already hear the girls chatting in the kitchen.

'Good morning,' Amy and Clare both chimed.

'Morning.' I grinned. 'You're up early.'

'We wanted to get your breakfast ready for when you came down,' Amy said, presenting me with a continental breakfast, complete with fresh croissants, bread, jams, cheeses, hams and a cup of coffee.

'Oh girls, you are both absolute angels. Thank you,' I said, sitting down and tucking in. 'Mmmm, these croissants are delicious.'

'Clare baked them,' Amy said proudly.

'Really? Gosh, you could market them.'

Clare grinned. 'It's the latest thing we learned in college.'

'You're really enjoying it, aren't you?' I asked her.

'Yes, I can't wait to open my – our – own café, eventually.' She smiled at Amy.

'So that's the grand plan, is it?'

They both nodded, sitting down beside me with cups of tea in their hands. 'Yes, we're thinking of opening a place that sells mostly healthy food. You know, options for people with allergies and intolerances. Gluten-free, lactose-free, nut-free, etcetera,' Clare enthused before Amy interrupted.

'And we've got a fab name for it already.'

Both girls looked at each other as I raised my eyebrows, waiting to hear.

'Good Intentions,' they said together, excitedly.

'Oh wow, that's a fabulous name. Have you spoken to Adam about this? I'm sure he'd be keen to be involved, somehow. I bet he'd like to invest in you.' I smiled, taking a swig of my coffee.

'Do you really think so, Eve?' asked Clare.

'Absolutely. I'm amazed you managed to keep it a secret until now.'

'We'll speak to him when you get back from your honeymoon.' Amy winked. 'Do you know where you're going yet?'

I laughed and shook my head. 'No, but I have a good idea.'

'Where, where do you think?' Amy asked excitedly.

'I'm not saying, in case I'm wrong,' I laughed as I pushed the empty plate away from me. 'That was delicious, thank you, girls.'

The sound of a child crying interrupted us, and Clare stood up. 'I'll go and get her.' She smiled, taking a slice of toast and biting into it as she walked out of the room.

'I've got something for you,' Amy smiled, standing and nipping out of the room for a moment. She returned with a blue velvet box. 'I'd like this to be your borrowed,' she said, handing it to me. 'Provided you like it, of course.'

I opened the box and gasped at the most exquisite yet delicate diamond necklace. It was very simple, with little diamonds all over it.

'It's absolutely beautiful, Amy. Are you sure you want me to wear it?'

Amy nodded enthusiastically. 'It belonged to Nana Grove. She left it to me in her will.'

'Oh, Amy. I'm absolutely honoured, honey.' Tears threatened to fall, and Amy chuckled before she leaned forward and hugged me.

'It's my pleasure. You're my second mum, Eve, and you mean an awful lot to me, Clare, Junior, Jack, and Dad, of course. I'm thrilled you're marrying him.'

I wiped my eyes and sniffed loudly. 'How did I get so lucky?' I sighed. Most stepdaughters can't stand their father's new wife.' I laughed.

'Well, I'm not most stepdaughters. I'm Adam's daughter, and that makes me very different from most other girls.' She grinned as I stood up and hugged her again.

'You certainly are.'

oOo

I SAT in a chair while the stylist finished curling my hair into ringlets, before she gently loosened them with her fingers, pinning a few of them up and putting the small diamanté clip in place, showering me with hairspray.

'Not too much,' I laughed. 'I don't want rigid hair.'

She smiled and lowered the can. 'Sorry, I get carried away, sometimes. There, I think my job is done. What do you think?'

I turned to look in the mirror and smiled. 'It's perfect. Thank you.'

'Makeup,' shouted Amy from beside me, standing in a satin dressing gown, holding two glasses of Champagne. 'Here you go,' she said, handing one to me.

I took a long sip and relaxed into the chair while I waited for the makeup artist to come up the stairs. 'This really is wonderful,' I sighed.

Amy grinned and clinked glasses with mine. 'It is, isn't it? I just wish Mum could have been here.'

'Me too. Here's to you, Lisa,' I said clinking glasses again before taking another sip.

'I'm here, I'm here. Sorry. I hope I'm not late,' said the young woman with black hair with red highlights.

'No, right on time.' I smiled as she proceeded to work her magic on my face, using just a hint of tinted moisturiser before the blusher and then the eyes. It was the eyes I wanted a little more accentuated than usual. My lips would be just a shade darker than my natural colour, considering the lipstick would probably have disappeared within an hour of the proceedings, what with all the kissing and drinking Champagne I'd be doing.

'I think,' she said, adding a touch more mascara, 'I've finished. And you look strikingly beautiful if I do say so myself. Oh, I am good,' she giggled.

Looking into the mirror, I actually gasped at my reflection. The hair and the makeup made me look like someone from a Hollywood premiere. I couldn't wait to get into my dress!

'Wow, you're amazing. Totally amazing. Thank you so much. I'm delighted.'

'If you're delighted, then I'm delighted. Thank you for letting me do your makeup, Eve,' she said, air-kissing me so as not to smudge her work.

'Thank Clare and Amy. They were the ones that recommended you, said you were 'freaking awesome', I believe it was.'

'Aww really? Aww girls,' she said, turning to them and hugging them both.

'We always said at school that you would make an amazing makeup artist. I'm just so glad you're following your dream, Cat.'

She squeezed them both tight. 'Thank you. Right, I'd better be going. I've got another wedding to do this morning.'

'Fantastic. It's obviously really taking off now?' Clare said, helping her with her makeup bags.

'It is, and this one is for someone semi-famous,' Cat whispered, 'so it could mean more work in the future for all her mates.'

'Oooh, lovely. Good luck, Cat,' I shouted as she disappeared out of the room.

'You really do look amazing, you know. Dad is going to, well... he's going to be blown away, Eve.'

I smiled. 'Thank you.'

She turned to close the door. 'Right, I'll leave you to get dressed. Give us a shout if you need any help.'

'Will do,' I said nervously. I was so excited to get into the dress hanging up in a special bag on the back of the door.

I slowly unzipped it and grinned like a Cheshire cat. It was my dream dress; I couldn't quite believe that it was mine.

Letting the dressing gown drop to the floor, I took off the simple cotton knickers I'd been wearing since having a shower earlier and replaced them with the new grey smooth silk ones I'd bought for the occasion. I put on the matching strapless bra and grinned wickedly, remembering the kinky lingerie I'd bought for later.

Taking the dress off the hanger, I very carefully stepped into it. I just about managed to do up the zip but struggled at the top, so I called out to the girls who pushed open the door and slowly tiptoed in.

'Oh my God,' Clare said, her mouth opening. 'You look fucking amazing,' she said, not even thinking about the language she was using.

I laughed. 'Fucking amazing?'

She put her hand over her mouth. 'Did I just say that out loud?'

'Yes, babe, you did,' Amy laughed. 'But you're right. Have you ever seen anyone so beautiful?'

Clare shook her head. 'Only you, of course,' she laughed.

Once they'd fully zipped me up, I took a breath and then stepped out in front of the mirror. It literally took my breath away.

'Oh,' I said shivering.

'You cold?' asked Amy.

'No, not at all. I just got a shiver, that's all.'

'Yeah, that's what happens when your aura glows the amount it's glowing right now, Eve. You are absolutely stunning.'

'You really think so?' I asked.

'We seriously know so,' Amy replied. 'What do you think?'

'I love it. I really, really love it.'

The soft grey lace clung to me in all the right places, hugging my hips, thighs, waist and breasts, the dress flared out just above the knee. A black sash accentuated my little waist. As I turned around, the back was open at the top, revealing just the right amount of skin and the sleeves covered my arms, perfect for an

English spring wedding. To top it all off, I had a small black fur bolero for when we were outside. I couldn't stop smiling.

'Oh, we nearly forgot,' Amy scrambled out of the room, returning with a large box. 'This is from Dad.'

'Oh,' I said, wondering what it was.

I pulled and ripped at the wrapping paper until the box was visible and then I gasped loudly.

'What is it?' Amy asked. Both girls were on their knees next to me.

'Shoes?' Clare asked.

I nodded. 'Not just any shoes. Christian Louboutins. Black, I would imagine,' I said as I opened the box to find a card and the cotton bag I recognised from the Vancouver shop. I pulled it open and laughed. Yes. The shoes I'd tried on. The ultra-expensive shoes I'd tried on.

'Oh my God,' I whispered.

Amy took the shoes out of the bag as I read the card.

Dearest Eve,

You probably knew I was acting strangely after you'd tried these on. Well, you were right. I was trying to buy them behind your back. I arranged for them to be sent from Canada. Unfortunately, there was a slight delay with customs, and so I thought they'd make a nice little wedding gift. You don't have to wear them. I know you said they were rather high! But you could always wear them for the ceremony and change for the reception?

I am so honoured to be a part of your life, Eve. And I am incredibly excited at the prospect of becoming your husband. I want to make you happy. That is my purpose in life now. You and the kids are all that matters. I love you.

Your soon to be husband,

Adam.

Tears threatened to fall.

'Oh no,' Clare said, rushing towards me with a tissue in hand. 'Don't cry. Don't you cry now.'

I smiled and took the tissue gratefully, dabbing at my eyes with it.

'I think you'll find Cat used waterproof makeup, so you'll be alright,' Amy said as she held the shoes out to me. 'Are you going to wear them?'

'I'd like to, but they might be a little high for this dress. Oh what the hell, I'll wear them anyway,' I said, as I sat back down and put the first one on, sighing happily. The second one, I started to slide my foot inside, but it wouldn't go any further, so I pulled it off and peered into it.

Inside was a small velvet bag.

'What's this?' I grinned, taking it out.

Clare elbowed Amy, and they both grinned.

'What?' I asked puzzled until I opened the bag, and a bracelet fell out.

'Oh goodness,' I cried.

'Dad had it made to match my necklace, which is only borrowed, but the bracelet is his proper wedding gift to you.' Amy grinned as she helped me put it on.

'It's perfect,' I breathed, looking at the twinkling diamonds.

'It cost a small fortune, so don't lose it,' Amy laughed.

'Amy!' Clare shook her head.

'What? Well, it did.'

oOo

TAKING A DEEP BREATH, I smiled as I started to walk down the stairs where Mum and Dad were waiting. Although she'd wanted to help me get dressed, I'd wanted to surprise her, so she relented and chilled out downstairs, drinking Champagne with a few old friends.

As I carefully descended in my new shoes, I felt like a million dollars.

A door opened, and they walked out into the hall, one by one, their heads lifted to look at me in all my splendour.

'Oh my,' Mum said, choking up. 'You look absolutely incredible. You'd give those Hollywood starlets a run for their money, love,' she added, dabbing at her eyes with a white handkerchief.

Dad was wearing sunglasses indoors, so I laughed at him.

'Oh Dad, you're not going to wear them all day are you?'

He was trying hard not to cry. I could tell by his quivering lips. 'Evelyn. I've never seen such beauty. You are a sight to behold, my love. Beautiful, absolutely beautiful,' he leaned forward as I reached the bottom of the stairs and kissed me on the cheek.

'Careful with her makeup, dear,' Mum said, air-kissing me and squeezing my hand.

'Mum, you look gorgeous too,' I said, checking out the perfectly chosen colour scheme for her skin tone. The burgundy red trouser suit and pale grey blouse made her glow. I particularly loved that she'd chosen a grey top to match with my dress. Turning her around so I could admire her long white hair, I noticed she had it up in a glamorous chignon.

She smiled at me as she patted the back of her hair. 'Your stylist did it for me before she left. She's very good.'

'She certainly is. She's done a fabulous job. I wonder if you'll be able to do it yourself?'

'I asked her for step by step instructions, which she gave me, so we'll see. If not, I'll just take the photos to my hairdresser in Portugal, and she can do it for me,' she smiled. 'Doesn't your father look dapper in his suit?' she said, admiring the man she'd been married to for fifty years.

'He looks so handsome. Did you choose the suit, Mum?' I asked as I watched him turn around with a little grin.

'Surprisingly, no. He chose it himself,' she said proudly.

'Wow, Dad. It's perfect. I love that colour on you.'

The dark grey pinstripe complemented his thick, dark grey hair perfectly. Dad had always been a handsome man, and I could see that would never change. Not even now, in his late sixties.

'Where are the girls, love?' Mum asked, eager to spend time with her newly acquired grandchildren and great grandchild.

I smiled. 'They're just getting dressed. They'll be down soon,' I said, turning my attention to a few of the girls I'd been to school with and kept in touch with over the years. They rushed forward and hugged me, telling me all the right things. We still had a little time until we were due to leave, so we headed back into the drawing room for another glass of Champagne, waiting for the girls to get ready.

Soon enough, I heard the door open and in they walked. I caught my breath.

Amy and Clare were both wearing floor length black satin dresses with a simple grey sash at the waist. The dresses were strapless, but both wore red fur boleros to match mine. They looked stunning. Amy's dark curls were up in a delicate plait, and Clare's short hair was, well, short and simple. Both wore a little tiara.

'You both look a million dollars,' I said, rushing towards them and hugging each one, careful not to squash the most adorable baby in Amy's arms, who wore the cutest black and grey dress with red hearts all over it.

'Do you like it?' Clare asked, spinning around.

'Yes, very much. I think the dress is perfect on you both. I hope you're okay about it. I know you're really not a dress kind of girl, Clare,' I laughed, frowning a little.

'For you, anything,' she said, hugging me. 'Besides, I look kinda hot.' She grinned.

'You certainly do,' Amy winked. 'And I know you like it on me, you were trying to take it straight off upstairs.' She laughed.

'Too much information,' I said, laughing as the photographer continued to pester us to pose together, on our own, each with the baby, with Mum and Dad.

Before we knew it, the cars had arrived, and we were climbing in. Mum, Dad and I were in the black Bentley decorated with grey lace, while the others were in a limo. All organised by Jack. I grinned, thinking about what he and Adam were going to look like in their snazzy suits.

CHAPTER 38

*M*um gave me a brief hug and then rushed off into the church as Dad, and I stopped for a moment, waiting for my gorgeous bridesmaids to walk on ahead.

'You ready, Angel?' he asked, squeezing my hand tight.

'I've never been more ready for anything in my life, Dad.'

'That makes me so happy, love,' he said as he readjusted his sunglasses.

'Dad, are you really going to keep them on in church?' I asked, smiling.

He sniffed loudly and nodded. He was quite a shy man and clearly didn't want everyone to see his teary eyes.

'That's ok. You can keep them on,' I squeezed his hand and kissed him on the cheek. 'I love you, Dad.'

'I love you, angel,' he whispered as the music began.

The sounds of Sade's Your Love Is King echoed throughout the little church as Dad looked at me with a grin, and we started walking slowly down the aisle towards the love of my life.

I watched Adam turn as we entered the room, and he visibly gasped before grinning and nodding his head at the sight of me.

I couldn't take my eyes off him, not even for a second. Not until Dad and I reached him when I smiled at my father. He gave me a kiss and stepped aside, going back to sit beside Mum, who I knew was probably bawling her eyes out – albeit silently. Adam reached out to me, and we held hands throughout the whole ceremony, where we promised to love and cherish each other. I didn't fancy having to obey him, so we omitted that part by mutual consent.

We exchanged rings, and both of us smiled widely at the memory of choosing the diamond bands a few months earlier. And then it was the moment we'd been waiting for. It was the moment that made it official (after signing the necessary paperwork, that is), the moment the vicar said, 'I now pronounce you husband and wife. Adam, you may kiss your bride.'

Whoops and sounds of joy rang out from around the church as all our friends and family jumped up and yelled, clapping and laughing as Adam dipped me backwards and planted the most delicious kiss on my lips, which lasted a trifle longer than it probably should have done in a place of worship. But it added to the atmosphere, making everyone laugh and me dizzy with emotion.

As we walked towards the entrance of the church, we stopped and stood waiting for all our guests to get up and follow us out, where we greeted them all briefly, kissing, hugging, them congratulating us.

Matt and Charlie were the last to appear, and both looked emotional but delighted. I couldn't help but notice that she kept putting her hand absent-mindedly on her belly.

'When are you due?' I whispered into her ear.

'How did you know?' she exclaimed.

I pointed to her hand, which was firmly over her belly again.

'Oh, it's becoming a habit, I guess. August, the middle of the month, I think.'

I hugged her. 'Congratulations,' I said before I hugged Matt tightly too. 'I'm delighted you're having more babies,' I whispered to him. 'You deserve to be happy.'

'We both do.' He grinned.

'See you at the reception,' they said, as they disappeared outside.

Just before we were about to step outside, Adam pulled me to him and hugged me.

'I can't quite believe that we're married,' he whispered.

'I know, me too.'

We walked out, hand in hand, and thousands of rose petals descended on us as we walked through the crowd and climbed into the Bentley, where Adam kissed me deeply, pulling me even closer to him.

'You are the most exquisite bride, Evie. The most beautiful woman I've ever seen. You look like you should be in a Hollywood movie.'

I chuckled. 'Mum pretty much said the same thing. Thank you, husband. You look pretty hot yourself, in that suit.'

He wore a grey three-piece suit with a pale grey shirt and a red cravat, which made his dark exotic eyes pop. He was so handsome, I could quite easily have taken him there and then.

'Why thank you, wife,' he said, taking my hand to his lips and gently kissing it as we drove for a while, making sure that we arrived after all our guests.

Once we were sure enough time had passed, we drove down the long winding country road that led to the reception, which was to be held at an old large farmhouse and barn that had been converted into a hotel and reception venue. It was homely, beautiful and very traditionally English. Adam had loved it the moment we'd set eyes on it, and we were lucky enough to be able to book it at short notice.

As we pulled up outside the main entrance, all the guests stood waiting, drinking Champagne and Bucks Fizz, some of the men with beers in their hands – naturally.

Adam climbed out first and came round to my side to help me out, like a true gentleman, while the photographer clicked away. We grinned as we were led away from the wedding guests so he could do his job. Soon we were joined by our bridesmaids and best man, Jack, who looked like a movie star himself in his suit that matched his father's.

We had loads of photos taken in stylish and amusing poses outside before taking more indoors with all our guests and family members, and then it was time to eat. I knew I was starving, and everybody else must have been famished too.

We ate roast meats and steamed salmon with a multitude of delicious fresh vegetables, many of which were grown on the grounds of the property before delving into the most delicious English puddings.

Before we knew it, it was time for the speeches. Waiters and waitresses rushed around, clearing the tables and placing several bottles of Champagne on each one. Jack stood up first, carefully tapping his spoon against his glass, making sure he had everyone's attention.

'Hello everyone,' he said confidently. 'Thank you all for coming. It's wonderful to see so many old and new friends. I was so honoured to have been offered the job of being the best man today for my father. I'm not sure what he was thinking, to be honest, considering the first time I ever laid eyes on his beautiful new wife was when I accidentally walked in on them enjoying a little nookie!'

Embarrassed, I covered my mouth with my hand as everyone chuckled. I avoided looking at Mum.

'But, aside from that minor indiscretion,' everyone laughed again, 'I don't have any jokes or anything bad to say about the two of them. I adore my father, I always have. I know he's made some unusual choices in his life before,' he searched the sea of faces until his gaze rested on Charlie's, to whom he nodded his head, and some people chuckled. Charlie stuck out her tongue, causing a few more to laugh under their breath. 'But none have ended too badly. I mean, his ex-wife is a guest today, and she recently married Eve's ex-husband, which is all a little odd, to say the least, but they're all happy and that, really, folks, is all that matters, right?'

'Hear, hear,' said a few people.

'Eve has been a real godsend to us. Ever since she came into our lives, she has proven herself to be the love of Dad's life. She accepted us all for who we truly are,' he said, looking over at his sister and Clare with love, 'and helped us through a particularly horrendous time. I know my mother was very fond of her, and that made me look at her in a new light. I must admit that I struggled to accept the situation at first, but I was soon made to realise that Eve was always meant to be a part of this family, and I know that I'm looking forward to being a part of it with her. It's what Mum wanted, and it's what I want. It's what we all want,' he said, looking at Clare and Amy, who both nodded enthusiastically before he continued. 'Dad, you're a lucky man. Eve, you're a lucky woman, not just to get Dad, but to get all of us too.' He grinned. 'Everyone, please raise your glasses to the wonderful bride and groom,' he smiled.

Everybody did as he asked, as Adam stood up and hugged his son, and I did the same.

'Jack, thank you so much,' I whispered into his ear, wiping away a tear that threatened to fall down my cheek. 'That means so much to me.'

He squeezed my hand. 'I meant every word, Eve. I'm sorry it took me so long to come around. Welcome to the family,' he beamed as we both sat back down.

I felt such a sense of belonging and serenity.

Staying on his feet, Adam took the microphone from Jack and waited for his son to sit back down.

'Thank you, son,' he grinned. 'That was beautiful. I just wanted to say a quick thank you to you all for coming today. It has made it extra special to have you all here with us. Old friends and new, family members and children, we are truly blessed to have you all in our lives. I'd particularly like to thank all those of you that travelled overseas to be here; Portugal,' he said looking at my parents, grinning, before catching the eye of Flavia and Michele, owners of Onda Vicentina where I'd started to find myself again, 'Italy, France, South Africa and Australia, I believe. Thank you to my beautiful daughter, Amy, her partner, Clare, and their adorable baby girl, Lisa Junior, for being the bridesmaids today. You look astoundingly beautiful, and you make me so proud. Jack, my son. Thank you for being such a fabulous best man and for not leading me down a dodgy path during my stag night. I was so worried I'd end up naked and tied to a lamppost somewhere.' Everybody laughed while I shook my head. 'But no, they left me naked and tied in front of the local police station instead. No, I'm joking,' he laughed as my mother looked at him in wide-eyed shock before she shook her head and laughed. 'To Eve, thank you for walking back into my life when I needed you the most. It's been a rough ride for both of us, but you were always patient with me while I went through a tough time. You made me stronger. You made me want to be the best husband in the world, the best father I could possibly be, and now,' he glanced at little Lisa Junior, 'the best grandfather too. Gosh, I still can't quite get my head around that.' He grinned. 'Eve, you've made me the happiest man on Earth today. Words cannot describe how I feel about you, how much I love you, so I thought perhaps I could show you instead...'

Frowning, I looked up at him as he grabbed my hand and pulled me to my feet. Expecting him to kiss me, I was surprised when he pulled me to the dance floor, where he carefully lowered me into the single-seat which had been placed in the middle. I looked around and noticed a few people grinning. Adam walked away from me, and suddenly, music started playing. I looked around, trying to find him in the crowd that had developed at the sides of the dance floor. Suddenly, he appeared, with no shoes on. I covered my mouth with my hand and frowned, and then he ran and skidded on his socks so that he was next to me. In his hands were some large pieces of card.

He stood in front of me and held out the cards. The music changed to something really upbeat, and soon I could hear the sounds of Justin Timberlake all around me. Adam grinned and held out the first card.

AIN'T Nobody Love You Like I Love You

HE NODDED, moving his head to the music like Michael Jackson. I laughed while he threw the card away to reveal the second one that said,

WHEREVER YOU WILL GO I will Go

THE MUSIC suddenly slowed down so that it was now Wherever You Will Go by The Calling. I laughed again as he swooned, singing all the lyrics, moving his upper body side to side until the music changed again and he dropped that card to reveal another one that said,

I Love You Like Never Before

THE MUSIC SLOWED RIGHT DOWN, and I could hear the gentle tones of one of my favourite singers, Eva Cassidy. Adam slowly dropped the card and lifted me off the chair, twirling me around to the sounds of the beautiful song. I smiled, embarrassed as he softly kissed me on the cheek before he tenderly placed me back on the seat. I went to stand up, thinking that was the end but he shook his head and wagged his finger at me, gently pushing me back down.

Then all of a sudden, the music stopped. Nobody did a thing, they all just watched me sitting there. I turned to see them all smiling. When I turned back, Adam was gone. I chuckled. 'Where did he go?' I asked quietly.

Then some background music started up, and I grinned. I'd recognise that song anywhere. Suddenly the crowd parted, and Adam was standing there with an umbrella in his hand. He started walking around the dance floor before he began singing himself! Himself! I didn't know he was brave enough to sing in public. And then, before I knew what was happening, a couple of our guests were lifting my chair and moving me to the side of the dance floor.

I giggled as Adam moved towards the centre and started dancing, exactly like Gene Kelly in the movie. I couldn't stop laughing, and I was startled by Amy and Clare, who suddenly appeared, also carrying umbrellas, copying his dance routine. The icing on the cake was when Jack appeared behind them too. Then, about thirty of the guests started joining in, in some kind of rehearsed routine. I clapped my hands together joyfully, laughing and pointing. It was wonderful. As the song came to an end, Adam stopped singing and slowly walked towards me. The music stopped, and then another song began, and I threw back my head with laughter.

Marvin Gaye's Let's Get It On played loudly. Adam did a

shoulder roll and pouted at me before he stood before me and held out his hand.

'May I have this dance?' he asked. I nodded and jumped up from my seat as he led me to the dance floor. He dipped me before grinding his body against mine. The crowd whooped loudly and clapped, laughing as we danced playfully until the song finally came to an end, and the crowd cheered. I clapped and cheered too before my husband took a bow and then kissed me and twirled me around the dance floor. The next song started, and he beckoned others to join us to the sounds of Le Freak by Chic, a great 70s disco tune. The party had truly begun, and I knew that I would never forget it.

CHAPTER 39

'Don't you think it's time you told me where we're going?' I asked my new husband the next morning, enjoying breakfast on the worn-out hotel bed.

'I think you probably guessed ages ago, didn't you?' he replied, putting a strawberry into my mouth.

'I've had some ideas, yes.'

'So where do you think I'm taking you for our honeymoon?'

'Canada.' I grinned.

He laughed. 'Am I that obvious?'

'Sometimes.' I laughed as he elbowed me gently in the side.

'Where in Canada are we heading?' I asked, desperate to know where we were going the following day.

'Now that would be telling.'

'Come on, you can't leave me hanging.'

'I can...' He grinned. 'Unless you want to try and get it out of me.'

I moved the tray from the bed and jumped back on him, tickling him.

He shook his head. 'Sorry, I'm not ticklish enough. It'll take more than that to get it out of me.'

'Oooh,' I said, dropping the dressing gown from my shoulders and revealing my naked body beneath it. 'How about this?' I asked.

'Now we're getting somewhere,' he said, placing his finger on my shoulder and stroking it, using it to push the gown further down and then undoing the belt with both hands. He opened it with one finger and looked me up and down.

My breath caught in my throat just watching his face, looking at me so lustfully. I knelt so I could remove the gown altogether, throwing it to the floor. I inched closer to him, so his face was level with my chest. Lifting his hands to my side, he pulled me close so he could kiss my breasts. He opened his mouth and tugged at my nipple with his teeth, licking it, making me so wet. I groaned and leaned forward to remove his dressing-gown before I straddled him, hovering above him.

'Am I getting closer yet,' I whispered in his ear.

'Yes,' he answered breathlessly. 'You're almost there.' He smiled.

'Yes, I am,' I groaned louder and louder before I pulled back and lifted myself up so I could sit back down with him firmly inside me. He groaned really loudly, and I giggled.

'Sshhhh.'

Soon, we couldn't care less about the noise as I lay above him, grinding against him, groaning, enjoying every second, making love to my husband. We came together, shuddering, both covered in a light film of sweat.

'Wow,' he sighed. 'You're an amazing, woman, you know that?'

'You're not so bad yourself. Now, what were we talking about? Canada? I think I might have just, erm... fucked it out of you, right?'

Adam laughed and rolled over, looking at me. 'Okay, okay. Yes, you couldn't tickle it out of me, but fucking on the other hand... Fucking is good.' He grinned.

'So where are we going?'

He laughed and stood beside the bed with his hand outstretched. 'How about I tell you in the shower?'

'You're not going to tell me just yet though, are you? I have a feeling more fucking is required?'

'More fucking? Yes please,' he said, licking his lips as I followed him into the bathroom.

oOo

HE DIDN'T TELL me where we were going until we actually got to the airport, using it as the perfect excuse for more sex. Not that an excuse was needed, of course. I'd been so horny, especially since the wedding. It was his dance routine that did it. I hadn't been expecting it, and knowing that he'd been rehearsing it for months, with so many of the guests, made it all the more special.

'You okay?' he asked as the plane came in to land at Vancouver airport.

I rested my head against his shoulder and nodded. 'Couldn't be better,' I sighed.

'Good, because I have a surprise for you,' he said, as I lifted my head.

'Another one? It's been nothing but surprises the past few days.' I grinned.

'We're not actually staying in Vancouver. Not yet, anyway.'

'Oh, we're not?' I asked, intrigued.

He shook his head. 'We're taking a little trip, first.'

My eyes widened in anticipation.

'I wanted our honeymoon to be extra special, and I know that you have a thing for special scenery, so...' he said, pulling out a brochure from the bag he'd kept under the seat, and handing it to me.

'A cruise?' I asked, confused.

He pointed to the brochure. 'Look closer,' he said.

'To Alaska?' I squealed. 'We're going to Alaska? Oh, my God. I can't believe it.'

Adam laughed. 'I wanted to take you somewhere unique, and when I enquired at the travel agency, they said that from Vancouver, this was the best trip to do. I hope I made the right decision?'

'The right decision? Oh my God, Adam. I've always wanted to go somewhere like that. I'm so excited I could die.'

'Oh, don't do that,' Adam smiled. 'Whatever you do, don't do that. I want you to stay with me until I'm ready to die too. And I'm not ready. Not today.' He smiled, stroking my face.

'Oh, Adam. I love you so much.'

'I love you too, and I have a feeling that fate hasn't finished with us just yet.'

THE END

FREE DOWNLOAD

Willow Tree Farm

Nestled among a thicket of weeping willows deep in the heart of Dartmoor, lies a house like no other. A house defying the laws of logic—and gravity for that matter. Some might even say it had a mind of its own. They wouldn't be wrong.

Affectionately known as Willow, this house has been an integral part of the Winterbourne family for over 400 years, and it is very, very protective of the Winterbournes, so woe betide anyone who dares to wrong this family of witches…

Compatible with all reading devices.

Exclusively available, and never before published.

Get your FREE COPY of Willow Tree Farm when you sign up to the author's VIP mailing list. **Get started here:**

www.suzyturner.com/free-book

ABOUT THE AUTHOR

Suzy Turner wrote her first chick lit novel in her early twenties, but it wasn't until much later that she decided to focus on writing full time. It was during a visit to Canada in 2009 when the ravens within the dark eerie forests of British Columbia called to her. The story of Lilly Taylor was born soon after and the first novel in The Raven Witch Saga was created. Suzy has since published several more urban fantasy books (under her pen name SG Turner) and contemporary women's novels.

Having lived in Portugal since childhood, Suzy, who is originally from Yorkshire in England, loves to travel. She finds inspiration wherever she goes. Old decrepit buildings, graveyards, cathedrals and castles are just a few of the things that can be found within the worlds of her urban fantasy books, and her contemporary women's fiction novels are filled with fun friendships, ordinary people in extraordinary circumstances and quirky characters you'd want as friends.

Suzy lives in the Algarve with her husband, three cats and a dog, where she practices yoga every morning and does 'bookish' stuff for pretty much the rest of the day!

For more books and updates, visit www.suzyturner.com

facebook.com/suzyturnerbooks
twitter.com/suzy_turner
instagram.com/suzyturner